PLAY ME A LOVE SONG

A lemon-colored moon hung over them in the cloudless sky. "I had a wonderful time," Liberty said softly.

Brent leaned toward her and tilted her chin up with his cupped hand. After staring into her eyes, he kissed her lips with a gentle caress that left her giddy.

"See you tomorrow morning," Brent whispered. Then he kissed her again lightly on the cheek, climbed into his pickup, and drove away.

Liberty hugged herself in ecstasy. Brent had kissed her, and she knew she would never be the same.

Bantam titles in the Sweet Dreams series. Ask your bookseller for any titles you have missed.

158.	CROSSED SIGNALS	175.	PUPPY LOVE
161.	MY PERFECT VALENTINE	176.	WRONG-WAY ROMANCE
162.	TRADING HEARTS	177.	THE TRUTH ABOUT LOVE
163.	MY DREAM GUY	178.	PROJECT BOYFRIEND
164.	PLAYING TO WIN	179.	RACING HEARTS
166.	THREE'S A CROWD	180.	OPPOSITES ATTRACT
167.	WORKING AT LOVE	181.	TIME OUT FOR LOVE
168.	DREAM DATE	182.	DOWN WITH LOVE
169.	GOLDEN GIRL	183.	THE REAL THING
170.	ROCK 'N' ROLL SWEETHEART	184.	TOO GOOD TO BE TRUE
171.	ACTING ON IMPULSE	185.	FOCUS ON LOVE
172.	SUN KISSED	186.	THAT CERTAIN FEELING
173.	MUSIC FROM THE HEART	187.	FAIR-WEATHER LOVE
174.	LOVE ON STRIKE	188.	PLAY ME A LOVE SONG

Sweet Dreams

PLAY ME
A LOVE
SONG

Bette Headapohl

BANTAM BOOKS
NEW YORK · TORONTO · LONDON · SYDNEY · AUCKLAND

PLAY ME A LOVE SONG
A BANTAM BOOK 0 553 29450 4

First publication in Great Britain

PRINTING HISTORY
Bantam edition published 1992

Cover photo by Pat Hill

Bantam Books are published by Transworld Publishers Ltd., 61–63 Uxbridge Road, Ealing, London W5 5SA, in Australia by Transworld Publishers (Australia) Pty. Ltd., 15–23 Helles Avenue, Moorebank, NSW 2170, and in New Zealand by Transworld Publishers (N.Z.) Ltd., 3 William Pickering Drive, Albany, Auckland.

Printed and bound in Great Britain by Cox & Wyman Ltd., Reading, Berks.

PLAY ME
A LOVE
SONG

Chapter One

"Lib, are you going to the beach party Saturday?"

Liberty Layton turned and gave her friend an incredulous look. "Are you kidding, Maribeth? Do you think I want more freckles than I already have?"

"Brent Miller will be there," Maribeth said with a knowing smile. Brent was a popular senior, a member of the student council, and an all-around hunk. Liberty thought he was cute, but she had never even spoken to him.

"I don't care if *Tom Cruise* is coming. I haven't forgotten that awful sunburn I got when I first moved here last summer. And now I have a thousand or so *more* freckles to show for it!"

"Maybe if you wore a lot of sunblock . . ." Maribeth offered hopefully.

Liberty shook her head. "No way. There isn't that much sunblock in the world! My only hope would be to wear a full-length muumuu, and I doubt that would impress Brent very much . . . not that I care what he thinks," she added hastily.

The January afternoon was unseasonably warm, and a soft breeze ruffled Liberty's shoulder-length blond hair as she and Maribeth passed through Grover Cleveland High's main entrance on their way outside. *Back in Indiana the ground is probably covered with snow*, Liberty thought.

"Are *you* going to the beach party?" she suddenly asked Maribeth, forcing her thoughts away from the life and friends she had left behind.

Maribeth sighed. "I'd hate to go without you. But I'd hate *not* to go, too, even though every swimsuit I own makes me look like a pear."

After they had boarded the bus and found two seats together, Liberty sat and gazed out the window, ignoring the high-spirited talk and laughter of the other kids around her. In the five short months since Liberty, her mother, and her grandmother had moved to San Diego from Smithdale, Indiana, Maribeth Anderson had become Liberty's best friend. She was the first person Liberty had met, and the two girls had hit it off immediately. Liberty hated to think of how lost she would be at Cleveland High without Maribeth. It was such a huge school—nothing like the small-town high school she had attended in Smithdale. Liberty had dozens of friends there. But at Cleveland, there seemed to be so many cliques that made little room for outsiders.

Maribeth nudged Liberty gently. "Earth to Liberty. Come in please!"

Liberty blinked. "Oh—sorry, Maribeth. I was just thinking . . ."

"Homesick again?"

"Yeah, kind of," Liberty admitted. "San

Diego is so—so different after living in a small town."

"That's another reason you should go to the beach party," Maribeth pointed out. "It'll take your mind off being homesick."

"I don't know, Maribeth," Liberty said. "All that sun . . ."

"You could wear a cover-up. And it probably won't be too hot. Last year it was freezing for the party."

Liberty sighed. "I'll think about it," she promised Maribeth as they got off the bus and walked to the town house complex where they both lived.

As they went their separate ways, Liberty noticed the brightly colored flowers in bloom everywhere. *It's hard to believe it's winter*, she thought. On the way to her building, Liberty passed the swimming pool. It was full of noisy swimmers and surrounded by sunbathers, and the strong smell of chlorine filled the air. *San Diego doesn't even smell like winter!*

Before entering her home, Liberty deliberately stood up straight and squared her shoulders. Her mother had always encouraged her to be proud of her height. It wasn't so bad now—a lot of the guys her age were taller than her own five feet ten—but back in grade school it had been awful. Liberty had been the tallest person in her class, and sometimes she still found herself slumping to make herself look smaller.

"We're going to have a really early dinner," her mother said, coming out of the kitchen with a huge bowl of salad in her hands. "I have to leave for the airport in an hour—I have three interviews in Seattle tomorrow."

Her mother's job involved interviewing and evaluating people who were applying for management positions in a national hotel chain. She was often gone for several days at a time, and since her promotion and the family's move to the West Coast, her responsibilities had greatly increased.

Liberty's heart sank as she followed her mother into the dining area. "How long will you be gone?" she asked.

"Just a few days. You and Gram can manage, can't you?"

"Sure," Liberty said noncommittally. "We always do, don't we? Where's Gram?"

"Can't you smell that heavenly chicken? She's out on the patio charbroiling."

Just then the patio door slid open and Liberty's grandmother peered inside. "Is that my favorite granddaughter, home after a day of fun and frolic at Cleveland High? Meet any hunks today?" she teased.

"Ha!" Liberty said as she took the platter of chicken her grandmother was carrying. "No such luck! Besides, all the real hunks are already spoken for."

"And I thought being a teenager was rough when I was growing up a hundred years ago," Gram said with an exaggerated sigh.

Liberty smiled and her heart grew warm with love. Though she missed having a father, Liberty loved her family. Especially Gram— she had always been there for her. But Liberty often wondered how different her life would have been if her dad, a classical guitarist, hadn't been killed ten years ago in an airplane crash on his way to a concert. If he were alive today, they would probably still be living in Smithdale, and Liberty would be looking forward to graduating from high school next year with the friends she had known all her life.

At dinner, Liberty asked the question that had been bothering her since Christmas. "You will be home for my seventeenth birthday in two weeks, won't you, Mom? Or are they sending you to Alaska or some other far corner of the world?"

Liberty and Gram had spent the holiday alone because Mrs. Layton's plane had been grounded in Chicago due to mechanical difficulties. Liberty had resented this, thinking that her mother surely could have made it home if she had really tried.

"I'll be going to Boston that week, but I'll definitely be home for the big day," Mrs. Layton assured her daughter, "even if I have to come by dogsled!"

After dinner, as Liberty stacked the dishwasher, she fought back the feeling of anger that always threatened to overwhelm her whenever her mother left on one of her business trips.

"Do you want to ride along with us to the airport, Lib?" Gram said, wiping the countertop with a damp paper towel.

Liberty shook her head. "No—I'd better get started on my homework," she said.

Later on in her room, Liberty lay on her

bed, her English book open but unread. Her mother, dressed in a navy blue business suit, stood in the open doorway with a concerned expression on her face. "We're leaving now, Liberty," she said. "Are you sure you don't want to come to the airport?"

"No, Mom. I have too much homework. Have a nice trip." She picked up the English book and turned a page, pretending to be absorbed in its contents.

"Okay, honey. See you when I get back on Sunday night," Mrs. Layton said. Liberty could hear the disappointment in her mother's voice. "Have a good week at school."

Liberty nodded silently.

When she heard the garage door close a few minutes later, she went to the kitchen and opened a can of soda. She didn't like shutting her mother out that way, but she couldn't help feeling angry and hurt. Because her mom had accepted the promotion and transfer, Liberty would probably never see her old friends again. She would never fit in at Cleveland the way she had back home. Her life was ruined, and all because her mother thought a raise and a promotion were more important than her own daughter's happiness!

Liberty finished her soda, then went back to her bedroom and took her old guitar out of its case. She strummed it idly, letting the music ease away some of her pain. Since the move to California, her guitar remained in the closet most of the time, much to her mother's disappointment. Mrs. Layton had hoped that Liberty would follow in her father's footsteps as a classical guitarist, and so had Liberty once. But her ambition seemed to be left behind in Smithdale, along with so many other things.

Gram may have accepted having our lives turned upside down, Liberty thought, *but I'm not going to adjust so easily.*

"Did you ask your mother about the beach party?" Maribeth asked Liberty as they walked to the bus stop the next morning. The air was crisp, hinting at cooler weather to come.

Liberty shrugged. "I forgot. It wouldn't matter anyway because she's out of town until Sunday night."

"Oh." Maribeth's face showed her disappointment. "So does that mean you're not going?"

"I don't know. It would mean leaving Gram home alone all day Saturday, and I don't like to do that."

"Yeah, I understand. Your grandmother's a neat lady."

They walked in silence for a few minutes.

"Steve Albers told Larry Wilson that Brent Miller thinks you're cool," Maribeth blurted suddenly as they turned the corner of a palm-lined street.

Liberty stopped in midstride, her brown eyes widening in amazement. "What? Are you serious, Maribeth? I didn't even think he knew I was alive!" She hugged her pile of books tightly, too astonished to move.

"I think he has a definite weakness for blondes," Maribeth said.

Liberty came back to earth. "Isn't he going steady with Margo Thompson?" Margo was a knockout blonde and she also was one of the most popular girls in the senior class.

"They just broke up—at least, that's the official rumor around school."

Well, thought Liberty as they entered Cleveland through the front doors, *that's interesting news.*

A few hours later, Liberty was on the cafeteria line when she became aware of someone towering over her. Turning, she looked up into the most beautiful pair of hazel eyes she had ever seen.

"Hi. I'm Brent Miller," the boy said. He reached for a tossed salad and smiled down at her. "You're new at Cleveland, aren't you?"

Liberty suddenly felt as if she couldn't breathe. If Brent was handsome from afar, he was absolutely devastating up close. She kept staring into those incredible eyes, searching frantically for something to say.

"Yes," she finally managed to reply. "I mean, no. I mean, I transferred here in October from a school in Indiana. That's where I used to live."

"Your name's Liberty, isn't it?" he asked with a warm smile that melted her bones to liquid butter. "That's an unusual name," Brent continued as he took an extra helping of fruit. "Were you born on the Fourth of July?"

"Everyone thinks that, but I'm an Aquarius." At his blank look, Liberty explained, "Aquarians are known for their independent attitudes and love of freedom."

Brent nodded. "I've got it now. Freedom—Liberty. That's cool."

"I'm just glad my parents didn't name me Free," Liberty said with a strained laugh. They had come to the end of the serving line, and they stood facing each other, holding their trays.

"Brent, hurry up," one of his friends called from a nearby table. "We saved you a seat."

"Yeah, coming," Brent responded, giving Liberty one more dazzling smile. "Are you going to the beach party Saturday?"

Gazing up into his hazel eyes, Liberty heard herself say, "Er—uh—yeah. Yeah, I'll be there."

"Great! I'll be looking forward to seeing you. Nice to meet you, Liberty."

Chapter Two

On Friday night, Liberty poked a French fry into a glob of catsup while Maribeth finished the last of a giant cheeseburger. Her own sandwich lay forgotten on a paper plate.

"No appetite?" Maribeth asked as she patted her lips with a paper napkin.

Liberty shook her head. "I'm more interested in finding a new swimsuit than in food. I just hope I can find one that doesn't make me look like I'm all arms and legs."

Maribeth giggled. "I wish *I* could be more interested in *anything* than in food. That'll be the day!"

After the girls were finished eating, they headed for the Fashion Valley Shopping Center to buy swimsuits for the beach party.

"Gee, this place is packed," Maribeth complained as she drove around looking for a parking space. Finally she found a place in one of the last rows. "We could have walked from home and been closer."

"The exercise will be good for us. It'll help burn off some of that junk food."

Maribeth cast an envious glance at Liberty's willowy figure. "You didn't eat enough to need to burn off anything. You want to look in here?" She pointed to the most expensive store in the center.

"No way, Maribeth!" Liberty exclaimed. "I don't want to spend my whole allowance. If my mother doesn't get me the sneakers I asked for for my birthday, I'll have to buy a pair later."

They walked on and finally went into Sports Stuff, a discount store that catered to teens and their budgets.

They each selected several suits, then headed for the dressing rooms.

Inside her little cubicle, Liberty tried on a

couple of swimsuits that did absolutely nothing for her. From the next room she heard a loud moan.

"What's wrong, Maribeth?" she called.

"Nothing, except I look like a sausage with arms and legs added as an afterthought!" Maribeth called back. "I'm going to buy a new beach robe and wear one of my old suits. No one is going to see this body but me, and I'm going to close my eyes from now on every time I pass a mirror!"

"What if it's really hot tomorrow? You can't hide in your robe all day," Liberty said as she slipped into a two-piece lime-green suit. She smiled at her reflection in the mirror. The suit was perfect, making her look as though she actually had some curves.

"It's supposed to turn cooler tonight," Maribeth said. "Looks like you worried about your freckles for nothing. Did you find anything?"

Both girls stepped out of their dressing rooms, and Maribeth gave a long whistle of appreciation. "You look great! I look like a cow!"

Liberty searched for the right words, not

wanting to hurt Maribeth's feelings. "If you'd just drop a few pounds, Maribeth," she said at last, "you'd look terrific. Not that you don't look nice now," she added quickly.

Maribeth gave a long sigh as she studied her round shape in the full-length mirror. "Don't kid me, Lib. It'd take more than a few pounds for me to look decent in a swimsuit— or anything else, for that matter." She patted her ample hips in disgust.

"Maybe I could help you lose some weight," Liberty offered.

"Yeah, right," Maribeth scoffed as they went back to their cubicles to change into their street clothes. "And how about a date with Mick Jagger while you're performing miracles?"

Liberty laughed. "He's too old for you. I'm serious. If you really want to lose, I'll help you."

"Well, maybe. I'll think about it," Maribeth replied.

After Liberty had paid for the green two-piece, she and Maribeth shopped for sales. Liberty found an oversize chrome-yellow shirt that would make a great cover-up, and she bought that, too.

On the way home, Liberty gave Maribeth some diet tips. "And remember, no more cheeseburgers or fries," she warned. "If you must have a hamburger, don't have it on a roll. Eat a small baked potato instead—*no sour cream.*"

Maribeth groaned as she turned into the drive of their town house complex and parked the car. "I never in my entire life had a baked potato without sour cream, cheese, and oodles of butter."

As she gathered her packages from the trunk of the car, Liberty broke into laughter. "You'll be surprised at how good a plain potato can taste when you're hungry. Besides, think of what you'll look like in a few weeks."

"Yeah—an undernourished sausage," Maribeth said glumly. "I'll pick you up around three tomorrow afternoon."

"Liberty, it's almost noon."

Her grandmother's voice penetrated Liberty's mind as she struggled to wake up the following morning. "Thanks for waking me, Gram. I probably would have slept right through the party," she said, stretching and yawning.

By the time Maribeth arrived, Liberty's stomach was tied in a nervous knot. She put on the yellow shirt, slipped into her thongs, and carried her beach bag and straw hat to the door where Maribeth, covered from head to toe by a bright pink terry cloth beach robe, greeted her. "Climb aboard, Annette. Frankie and the Beach Boys await," she teased.

"Bye, Gram," Liberty called. "I'll be home by about nine at the latest." She still felt a little guilty about leaving her grandmother all alone, but Gram had insisted it would be all right.

"Brrr," Liberty exclaimed as she stepped outside. The sky was overcast, and a chilly wind was blowing. "What happened to the weather?"

"I told you it was going to turn cool. San Diego weather is really unpredictable this time of year. Don't worry. You'll warm up at the beach, with all the fires for roasting hot dogs and stuff."

When they arrived, the beach was already crowded with what seemed like a million kids. Several volleyball nets had been strung up, and the shouts of the enthusiastic players rang up and down the beach. Liberty and Maribeth looked for a place to put their blankets and beach bags, and soon they found a patch of unoccupied sand.

By late afternoon the sun had managed to burn through the layer of clouds, adding an air of festivity to the party. Rock music blared from tape decks and radios, and couples danced on the warm sand. Munching on a hot dog, Liberty watched all the activity from the vantage point of her blanket. A huge boulder helped shield her from the sting of both the sun and the wind.

Liberty noticed that everyone gathered in cliques just as they did in school. And though she kept looking for Brent all afternoon, she couldn't find him anywhere.

"Want to play volleyball with us, Lib?" Maribeth asked.

Liberty peered through her sunglasses at a group of junior girls who were screaming and hitting a ball around down near the water.

"Thanks anyway, Maribeth," she said. "You go ahead. I think I'll just sit here for awhile."

Liberty watched Maribeth run to join her friends, and suddenly a great sense of loneliness swept over her. In spite of Maribeth, she felt isolated, unable to find the key that would admit her into one of those charmed circles of friendship. She shouldn't have come—Brent wasn't here, and it had obviously been a mistake to think she could fit in with his crowd. Behind her sunglasses Liberty's eyes misted. Back home in Smithdale, she had belonged. If only her mother hadn't—a deep voice interrupted her thoughts. "Hi, Liberty. Mind if I join you?"

As she looked up at Brent Miller, Liberty's cheeks became flushed and her heart gave a little flip-flop of delight. Wordlessly she moved over on the blanket to make room for him. He was dressed in jeans and a golden brown knit shirt that made flecks of metallic bronze dance in his eyes. Liberty could hardly believe that Brent had actually sought her out.

As they sat in silence watching the waves break on the rocky shore, Liberty searched frantically through the empty circuits of her mind for something—anything—to talk about. "You're not wearing a swimsuit," she blurted out.

Brent smiled. "That's because I came straight

here from my job. I work at a shoe store in the mall. I hoped you'd still be here."

At those words, Liberty's loneliness melted away. Did he mean he had come specifically to see her?

Brent went on. "So, do you like Cleveland High? What do you think of California?" He leaned back against the boulder, looking at Liberty with interest.

For some reason, Liberty suddenly decided to confide in him. Taking off her sunglasses, she said, "I—I feel out of place, I guess. I knew everyone in Smithdale, and at school."

"California seems pretty big and fast paced, is that it?" Brent asked.

She nodded. "I feel like one of those tiny fish at the bottom of an aquarium, the one that no one sees because it's hidden behind the castle or blends in with the seaweed. In Smithdale, I was more like—like a neon tetra!"

Brent smiled at her analogy. "It's gotta be tough, switching schools, especially in your junior or senior year. I guess you have to leave a lot of good memories behind, as well as a lot of friends."

Liberty felt the sudden sting of tears and quickly put her sunglasses back on.

He reached over and gently removed the glasses. "You have such beautiful brown eyes, like spiced cinnamon. It's a shame to hide them."

Liberty's heart took a wild tumble. For the first time in her life she didn't feel cheated because she had inherited her dad's brown eyes instead of her mother's blue ones.

As the deep orange sun sank behind the horizon, Brent took Liberty's hand and led her along the beach away from the noise of the party. The cool waves washed over their bare feet. Brent had rolled up his jeans and waded into the surf, pulling Liberty along with him.

"Isn't the sunset beautiful?" Liberty's voice was barely audible above the pounding of the waves.

"Yes," Brent agreed, squeezing her hand. "I'm glad I came, and I'm even more glad *you* came."

After their long, solitary walk they returned to the party and ate overcooked hot dogs and burnt marshmallows. But as Liberty eagerly anticipated what else the evening might bring, Brent suddenly glanced at his watch.

"It's been great, Liberty," he said, "but I have to go. I promised to meet someone, and I'm late."

The magic of the evening evaporated without warning. Liberty watched him roll down his pant legs and slip into his socks and jogging shoes. Had she done something to break the spell?

"I'll see you in school," Brent said, then walked briskly away.

Long after Brent had disappeared into the night, Liberty continued to gaze sadly down the beach.

Chapter Three

During the next two weeks, Liberty saw Brent often at school. He always waved and smiled, and once he even stopped to ask how she was doing, but there was a sense of strain between them that she simply couldn't understand. She relived that evening at the beach over and over, wondering what she had done or said to drive him away so suddenly. She knew she would never forget him holding her hand as they walked together in the surf.

A week before her birthday, the weather

turned warm again, making it seem more like July than February. The warm weather made it even more difficult to concentrate on schoolwork, and every night Liberty sprawled across her bed after dinner with her books open and her mind closed. Her thoughts would invariably drift to Brent, and she felt gloomier and lonelier than ever.

The night before her birthday, Gram and Liberty watched television as they waited for her mother to call from the airport. At nine-thirty Liberty glanced at the clock with a worried frown.

"Don't worry, dear," Gram said. "She's probably been delayed someplace. The weather is horrid in Boston."

"Don't they close the San Diego airport at eleven?"

Gram sighed. "I'm not sure, Lib."

Liberty stared at the television screen and sulked. She was certain that her mother wasn't going to make it home for her birthday. She and Gram would have to spend her big day alone—just like Christmas.

At ten-thirty the phone finally rang, and Liberty picked up the receiver.

"Hi, dear." Her mother's voice sounded muffled and far away.

"Hi, Mom," Liberty said coolly, trying to fight back her anger. "I can tell you're not at Lindbergh Field."

"No. I'm still in Boston. Everything is snowed in—no flights in or out for the next twenty-four hours. I'm sorry, sweetheart, but it looks like I'm not going to make it home for your birthday. I know you're upset, but—"

Liberty didn't wait to hear the rest. She handed the phone to her grandmother and went to her room, where she sprawled across the bed and stared out the window into the night. A few minutes later there was a light knock on her door.

"Come in, Gram."

"Liberty," her grandmother said sternly, sitting on the edge of the bed, "you were rude to your mother. You really hurt her feelings."

Liberty looked into Gram's disapproving eyes. "Oh, Gram, I'm sorry, but ever since Mom took this job she's never home. Her work means more to her than I do!" She burst into tears and buried her face in the pillow.

Gram sighed. "Liberty, deep in your heart, you know that isn't true. I want you to think about the way you've treated your mother for the past few months and try to see the situation from her viewpoint."

"Her viewpoint?" Liberty echoed, sitting up.

"Do you think you're the only one who has had to make sacrifices, Lib?" her grandmother asked. "Did it ever occur to you that it's been hard on your mother, too? She didn't want to move any more than you did, but her company offered her a lot more money along with the transfer and promotion. And before you start saying she thought the money was more important than your feelings, I want you to think about your mother's efforts for the past ten years. She's been supporting all three of us since your father died, and she's worried now about the cost of your college tuition."

Suddenly Liberty began to see things in a different light. "I guess you're right, Gram," she admitted. "I'm almost seventeen, and I've been acting like a selfish little kid."

Her grandmother smiled. "Yes, you have.

But if you just keep trying to look at this from your mom's perspective, you'll understand why she was so hurt when you behaved the way you did tonight." She kissed Liberty's cheek. "We'll talk more tomorrow, after you've had time to think."

Liberty woke up the next morning and went into the kitchen, where she found her grandmother frosting a chocolate cake.

"Happy birthday, Liberty," Gram said with a smile. "Ah, how I wish I were seventeen again and knew what I know now!"

"What would you do different, Gram?" Liberty asked.

"Not a single thing," she replied, her blue eyes twinkling in mischief. "How about a blueberry muffin for breakfast?"

Liberty sat at the kitchen counter nibbling a muffin while she watched her grandmother frost the cake. "Do you ever get lonely, Gram?" she asked suddenly.

Her grandmother hesitated a moment, then said, "I have you and your mother." She wiped her hands on her pink-flowered apron.

"I mean lonely for all your friends back home."

"Yes," Gram said. "I do miss my friends, my church, my clubs."

"Then why did you move way out here and leave all that behind? You could have stayed in Smithdale."

"Yes, I could have. But I felt you and your mother needed me," Gram said.

"You gave up all of your friends and your home just to be with us?" She slid off the stool and hugged her grandmother. "Thanks, Gram," she said softly, "for loving us so much."

After breakfast, Liberty opened her presents from Gram and gasped when she found fifty dollars tucked in her birthday card. "Oh, Gram, you shouldn't have," she said.

"And why not?" her grandmother said with a smile. "I can spoil my one and only granddaughter if I want to!"

That afternoon Liberty and Gram settled on the sofa to eat the birthday cake while they watched an old movie on TV. When the doorbell rang, she said, "I'll get it, Gram," and hurried to open the door. Maribeth stood there, looking guilty.

"Maribeth! Come on in," Liberty cried.

"I came by to let you know I blew it, and to bring your present," Maribeth said as she came into the living room.

"What do you mean, you blew it?" Liberty asked.

Maribeth sighed. "I mean I ate pizza, *lots* of pizza, last night."

Liberty laughed and hugged Maribeth. "Everybody's entitled to backslide now and then. Gram and I just had some birthday cake. Do you—"

"No way, José! Not even a crumb," Maribeth said virtuously. "Open your present now—it'll take my mind off of food."

Liberty opened the package and discovered a leather-bound book. "It's beautiful, Maribeth! Thank you." She smiled as she ran her fingers over the raised lettering on the cover that read, DREAMS AND THINGS. "I'll keep it on my nightstand and write all my dreams in it."

Then Maribeth asked, "Where's your mother?"

"She's snowed in at the airport in Boston," Liberty told her.

"Ah, that's too bad. I bet she's miserable

about missing your birthday. She probably feels terrible."

"Margery is good at making the best of a bad situation," Gram said. She glanced at Liberty. "Isn't that right, Lib?"

Liberty nodded. "Mom doesn't let much get her down." She and Gram smiled at each other. Then she turned to her friend. "Let's go for a walk, Maribeth. It'll help you work off that pizza. Do you want to come, Gram?"

Her grandmother settled back on the sofa. "Thank you, dear, but you girls run along and enjoy yourselves. I think I'll probably doze through the rest of this stimulating movie."

As they strolled through the town house complex, Maribeth asked, "Did you get those expensive sneakers you wanted, Lib? You sure gave your mother enough hints."

"I don't know," Liberty said. "I'm not going to open Mom's presents until she gets home."

As they left the grounds and headed downtown, the sun became even warmer.

"Want to take the bus?" Maribeth suggested hopefully.

"No way. You're going to repent for your sins, pizza-eater!"

Turning down a side street, they saw a man sprawled on the sidewalk by a garbage can. Despite the warm weather, he wore a dirty nylon parka and a wool cap pulled down over his ears.

"Do you suppose this is where he slept last night?" Liberty whispered to Maribeth.

The man peered at them through bloodshot eyes and scratched his gray beard. "Can you girls spare some change?" he mumbled.

Liberty quickly took a dollar bill from her wallet and handed it to him.

"Bless you, sweetheart." As he folded the bill and tucked it into his coat pocket, Maribeth pulled at Liberty's arm to drag her away. When they were out of hearing range, she said, "You know what he'll do with that money, don't you? He'll buy a bottle of cheap wine and drink himself into an alcoholic stupor."

Liberty turned to look back at the man, who was trying to hoist himself up by holding on to the garbage can. "Then at least maybe he can forget his troubles for a while," she said softly.

33

Maribeth let out a long sigh. "It's really terrible. There are so many people like that downtown lately."

After they had walked awhile longer, they approached an old building where a crowd was gathered outside the entrance.

"What's going on?" Liberty wondered aloud. She peered over Maribeth's shoulder to read the sign: FREE LUNCH DAILY FROM ELEVEN UNTIL TWO. "What a great idea!" she said. "Maybe we should go back and tell that man I gave the dollar to."

Maribeth shook her head. "He's not interested in eating, Lib, or he'd be here in line. This shelter tries to give everyone who's hungry at least one meal a day, even if it's only beans and rice. My mother gives money to it even though it irritates my dad. He always says homeless people could get a job if they really wanted to."

Liberty wondered how these unfortunate men and women could get a job. They had no presentable clothes; they needed baths and grooming. Who would hire them? Who would even interview them?

She and Maribeth walked around the long

line and were looking at an advertisement on the side of the building when suddenly a door opened and Brent Miller emerged, wearing a full-length white apron.

Liberty gasped. "Brent!" She was sure she must be dreaming.

He was just as surprised to see Liberty and Maribeth. "What are you two doing here in this end of town on a Saturday?" he asked.

"We were just out for a walk," Maribeth said. "We saw the crowd, and I was explaining to Lib what was happening."

Brent cast a worried glance at the long line. "Do you girls have any plans for the next couple of hours?"

"Not really," Liberty said, wondering what he had in mind.

"Could you possibly help out for a while? A couple of our regular volunteers didn't show up today, and we're really running behind schedule."

In less than five minutes Liberty and Maribeth found themselves in the serving line next to Brent as he gave them instructions on what and how much to serve each person. As the line moved endlessly by, Liberty forced herself to smile and tell each person to have a good day. At first she felt like a hypocrite because she knew most of them would be sleeping in a doorway, on the ground, or in a nearby park that night, but she soon found herself meaning it. And when she was rewarded with an occasional shy smile, it made her feel warm and wonderful inside. As soon as there was a momentary lull in the line, Maribeth excused herself to call her parents and Liberty's grandmother to let them know what they were doing.

Glancing around, Liberty noticed a guy with a video camera. He was taping a young woman who appeared to be interviewing some of the people in the shelter. She thought she recognized the woman as a reporter on a local television news program. *Good*, Liberty thought, *if they show this place on the news, maybe more people will realize how important it is to help the homeless.*

Just then, Brent lifted a tub of beans and placed it in front of her serving section. "How long have you been doing this type of work?" Liberty asked.

When Brent smiled at her, she felt strangely breathless.

"I started volunteering here about two years ago," he said. "Between this, my part-time job, and school, it gets a little hectic, but I feel a need to help people who don't even know where their next meal is coming from."

Liberty was really impressed. "Are you planning on a career in social work?" she asked.

"I wasn't until I started doing volunteer work here, but now that I realize how few people care about the homeless, I'm beginning to think I might. Hey, I really appreciate you and Maribeth helping out today," he added. "I guess I sort of pressed you into service without giving you much of a chance to make a getaway."

Liberty smiled. "I'm glad you did. I was feeling sorry for myself last night because my mother is snowed in back East and couldn't make it home for my birthday today. Now I realize how selfish that was."

"Well, happy birthday, Liberty. Glad I got to be a part of your big day." To her delight, he put an arm around her shoulders and gave her a hug, then added, "Working around here makes you learn not to feel sorry for yourself. You really learn to sort out your values."

After the last meal had been served, Brent drove Liberty and Maribeth home in his pickup truck. Liberty sat in the middle next to him, while Maribeth poked her head out the cab window and inhaled the fresh air.

"I don't care if I ever smell or see food again—especially beans!" she announced.

Chuckling, Brent said, "I want to thank you both for giving up part of your weekend. And especially you, Liberty, for working on your birthday."

"I enjoyed it," Liberty said shyly.

Brent let them out in front of the town house entrance.

"Thanks again, Liberty, Maribeth. I have to hit the freeway and get to my job at the mall. See you guys in school Monday."

Just before he drove off, Brent gave Liberty a special grin and said, "Happy birthday, Free!"

Chapter Four

"I'm sorry, Mom," Liberty said as she welcomed her mother home on Sunday. "I acted like a jerk on the phone the other night. I know you would have been here if you could have."

Her mother hugged her tightly. "Thanks, honey. Sitting around that airport for twenty-four hours was a nightmare—I'm really exhausted."

Liberty carried her mother's suitcase into the bedroom and turned down the covers on her bed. Mrs. Layton took off her wrinkled suit jacket and tossed it across a chair.

"Did you and Gram have a nice birthday celebration?" Mrs. Layton asked, stepping out of her heels and into fuzzy pink slippers.

"Not as nice as if you'd been here," Liberty admitted. Then she went on to tell her mother about working at the shelter.

When she had finished, Mrs. Layton smiled. "That was certainly an unusual way to spend part of your birthday, but I think it's terrific that you did it. And now we have some catching up to do. I want to give you your presents before I collapse!" She went to her closet and took out several brightly wrapped packages. "Happy birthday, dear," she said, handing them to Liberty.

Liberty was delighted with her gifts—a turquoise crocheted sweater, a book of classical guitar arrangements, and most of all, the very expensive sneakers she'd been hoping for. "Oh, Mom, thanks!" she cried, giving her mother a kiss. "They're absolutely perfect! Everything's perfect."

Mrs. Layton laughed. "I don't quite understand what's so special about those shoes, but if they make you happy . . ."

"They do," Liberty assured her. But it

wasn't just the shoes that made her feel so good, she realized as she carried her presents to her room. It was partly that, but it was also because for the first time in months she felt really close to her mother.

In her bedroom, Liberty tried to become absorbed in her homework, but Brent kept filtering into her mind. She wondered why she hadn't felt at all awkward with him at the shelter. Gazing out the window, she remembered everything they had talked about. He had really acted as if he liked her. Maybe she had just been imagining things when she thought he was avoiding her after the beach party. . . .

The shrill ring of the telephone snapped Liberty out of her daydream, and she grabbed it before it could awaken her mother, who had gone to bed exhausted from her long trip.

Maribeth's excited voice greeted her. "Lib, we're going to be on the six o'clock news!"

Liberty sat up. "What?"

"Didn't you see that cameraman at the shelter yesterday?"

"Come to think of it, I did," Liberty said. "But I didn't pay too much attention."

Maribeth giggled. "That's because you only had eyes for Brent!"

Liberty blushed. "That's not true. I was just too busy. Anyway, how do you know we're going to be on the news?"

"Because my mom saw a promo about it a few minutes ago on Channel 10. There was a picture of you, me, and Brent, dishing out rice and beans! Wait till the kids at school see it," Maribeth said. "We'll be famous! I hope I don't look too fat. Everybody says TV adds ten pounds."

"Vanity, thy name is Maribeth," Liberty teased. "Thanks for telling me. I'll tell Gram—Mom conked out a while ago."

At six o'clock Liberty turned on the local news. She and Gram waited eagerly for the human interest segment about the shelter. As they listened to the young woman Liberty had seen at the shelter talking about how wonderful it was that some teens were dedicated to helping others, Liberty felt embarrassed. Brent was dedicated, but she and Maribeth had only been there by chance.

They were on camera about half a minute, and the reporter had gotten Maribeth's last name wrong, calling her Andrews instead of Anderson.

"I looked horrible," Liberty wailed to her grandmother. "You could see all my freckles!"

"I thought you looked very nice," Gram said, "although I have to admit I was busy looking at that young man. He's very attractive."

The telephone rang, and Liberty hurried to answer it.

"Hi, celebrity," Maribeth said before Liberty could speak. "I thought I looked sooo fat! What did you think?"

Liberty twirled the curled telephone cord around her index finger. "It was so quick, Maribeth, I really didn't get a good look. To be honest, I was too horrified at my own appearance to pay much attention to yours!"

"At least Brent looked great, didn't he?" Maribeth asked.

Liberty let out her breath in a long, slow sigh. "Yeah. Even Gram thought so."

Liberty was unprepared for the number of people at school on Monday who had seen her on television. Even her social studies teacher commented on it, causing Liberty to turn bright pink as thirty pairs of eyes stared at her.

"You're to be complimented, Liberty," Mr. Moore said, adjusting his glasses. "Most of us tend to think only of ourselves and our immediate wants rather than of the needs of others."

Liberty felt a gnawing sense of guilt because she knew she was accepting praise that really belonged to Brent. If someone else had asked her to work at the shelter on her birthday, she probably wouldn't have done it.

"Sign a lot of autographs today?" Maribeth joked as she and Liberty changed into sweats in the girls' locker room after school. Liberty had talked Maribeth into jogging with her to shed some pounds.

"Amazing, wasn't it?" Liberty said, tying back her long hair. "All that attention kind of made me feel like an impostor. I mean, we were only there by accident. Brent's the one who deserves all the credit."

Maribeth dragged a brush through her

short, thick curls. "Yeah, you're right. But it's kind of fun being an instant celebrity anyway."

After they had locked their books and purses in their lockers, the girls headed for the athletic field.

"Gosh," Maribeth commented as Liberty did a series of deep knee bends, "it looks awfully big. How many laps are we going to do?"

"We'll start with two and go really slow, or your muscles will get sore," Liberty told her.

"I don't see why you're doing it, Lib. You don't need to lose any weight."

Liberty grinned. "Ever hear of muscle tone?"

They jogged in silence for several minutes. A few other kids who were working out waved as they passed.

"Doesn't that look like Brent over there with those other guys at the far end of the track?" Maribeth asked suddenly.

Liberty's heart somersaulted wildly as she looked in the direction that Maribeth was pointing. "I don't know—I can't see that far."

"When we get over there, if it is Brent, I'm going to leave you guys alone."

"No, don't," Liberty pleaded. "I'll get nervous and say something stupid—I just know I will!"

As they got closer, Liberty could see that it was indeed Brent talking to a group of senior boys. He waved and began walking toward her and Maribeth.

"Well, I'm beat," Maribeth said loudly. "I'm going to rest for a few minutes." She winked at Liberty and headed for a bench in the shade.

Liberty gazed into Brent's eyes, noticing how his navy sweats made his hazel eyes look almost blue.

"Hi, Lib," he said with a grin.

Liberty smiled. "Hi, Brent."

"Did you see us on the news?" he asked. "You looked great on the tube."

He thought I looked great? Liberty was delighted. "Maribeth told me it was going to be on," she said. "But I feel really funny about what they said about 'dedicated teens.' *You* deserve the praise, not Maribeth and me."

He fell into step beside her, and they began to walk slowly around the field. "I don't work there for praise, Lib. And your being there Saturday afternoon was really special. I enjoyed working with you very much. And Maribeth," he added quickly. He took her hand, and Liberty felt as though every cell in her body had been put on red alert.

Before she could think of anything to say, Brent continued, "I don't go to the movies often, but there's one at the Cineplex that I really want to see. Would you like to go with me Friday night? That is, if you don't have anything else planned, or another date or anything."

Dazed, Liberty whispered, "I'd love to go."

"It's an old French film—my psych teacher suggested seeing it." He smiled down at her. "At least if it's boring, I'll have good company."

Liberty didn't care if *The Three Stooges in Outer Space* was playing. Brent Miller had actually asked *her*, Liberty Layton, freckles, and all, for a date!

By the time they had circled the track to where Maribeth sat, Brent was glancing at his watch. "I have to run, Lib. It takes me half an hour to get to my job. I'll pick you up Friday about six, okay?"

"Fine," she agreed, and gazed dreamily after him as he walked away.

"Well?" Maribeth prompted as they headed back to the school. "If you don't tell me what's going on, I'm going to *explode!*"

"He asked me to a movie Friday night! I don't know what to wear. Should I wear a dress? Or jeans?"

Maribeth shook her head in amusement. "That's four days away, Lib. We'll have plenty of time to get you back in orbit by then."

Chapter Five

For the next four days, Liberty was unable to devote full attention to her schoolwork. She floated from class to class with a glazed look in her eyes. But when the final bell rang on Friday, nervous anticipation replaced her weeklong euphoria.

An hour later, Maribeth lay on Liberty's bed watching her frantically pull sweaters from the closet. Taking Maribeth's advice, she had decided to wear her best jeans for her date with Brent. But Liberty still hadn't decided on a top.

"What about this?" She held up a brown sweater with gold leather leaves appliquéd on the shoulders.

"Wow, that's hot! When I lose another twenty pounds, can I borrow it sometime?"

"Yes, but what about *me* for tonight? Remember?"

"Hold it up to your face. I don't know— what's that turquoise thing back there?"

Liberty tossed the brown sweater on the bed and pulled out the sweater her mother had given her for her birthday.

"That's gorgeous," Maribeth exclaimed. "It makes your skin look radiant."

Carrying the sweater into the bathroom's brighter light, Liberty held it up against her face. "Are you sure, Maribeth? Isn't it a little too bold?"

"What do you mean?"

Liberty said, "The color is so bright—this shade of blue kind of makes me feel like Bozo the Clown dressed for a three-ring circus."

"No, no, no," Maribeth insisted. "It makes you look dramatic. Besides, it goes better with those faded jeans than the brown one."

Having finally convinced Liberty to wear

the turquoise sweater, Maribeth left so that Liberty would have time to calm her nerves before Brent arrived. When she came into the living room at a quarter of six, her mother's eyes lit up with pleasure when she saw Liberty wearing her birthday present.

"You look beautiful, Lib."

Looking up from her needlepoint, Gram nodded in agreement. "I hope this Brent fellow realizes he's dating the prettiest girl in town."

"Oh, you're both prejudiced," Liberty protested, but inside she felt pleased. "You don't think I look too—too—you know, brassy?"

Her mother laughed. "Where did you ever get an idea like that? Is that why you wear so much olive-green and faded brown? I wear dark colors because they're more practical when I'm on the road. You're only seventeen—you don't have to be practical yet!"

Just then the doorbell rang, making Liberty jump. She took a deep breath and hurried to open the door.

She greeted Brent with a shy smile and brought him into the living room to meet her family. Gram and her mother seemed to be enchanted with him, and Liberty began to relax as she listened to Brent tell them about volunteering at the shelter and his aspirations to be a social worker.

"We won't be late," he told Mrs. Layton as they left. "I have to be at the shelter early tomorrow."

Alone with Brent, Liberty became nervous again. She wished that she could talk to him as easily as her mother and Gram had.

"You look awfully pretty tonight," Brent commented with a warm smile as they got into his pickup.

Liberty blushed and murmured "Thanks" as she fumbled with her seat belt.

Brent leaned over to help fasten her belt, and as his hand brushed hers, Liberty experienced that strange sensation of breathlessness.

The movie was in French with English subtitles, and Liberty found the plot difficult to follow, but she really didn't care. She glanced at Brent's profile in the dim theater light, and a shiver of pleasure rippled through her.

"Cold?" Brent whispered. Before she could

answer, he draped his arm around her shoulders and held her close to his side.

In his protective embrace, Liberty wished the movie could last forever. But it ended far too soon.

"So what did you think of it?" Brent asked as they walked out of the movie house.

"I'm not sure I understood it all," Liberty admitted.

Brent flashed a delighted smile and squeezed her hand. "Me either! I was afraid you were going to explain it to me and make me feel like a dope."

Squeezing his hand in return, Liberty laughed in disbelief. "*You* a dope?" Maribeth had told her that Brent was in the running for valedictorian of the senior class. How he managed to keep his grades up with all his extracurricular activities was beyond her comprehension.

They laughed as they climbed into Brent's truck and headed for Taco Joe's for Mexican food.

"Do you work at the shelter every Saturday?" Liberty asked later, taking a small bite of her chicken fajita.

"Yeah." Brent unwrapped his burrito and

added a full container of salsa. "More often in the summer. But I can only swing one day a week now, which is too bad because we're always a little shorthanded." He looked at her with a thoughtful expression. "Would you be interested in helping out? Do you have the time?"

Liberty was elated. If she volunteered at the shelter, she would be seeing Brent every weekend. And not just seeing him, but working and talking with him. "I—I think I could do it on Saturdays or Sundays," she told him.

"Terrific! Can you come tomorrow? I could pick you up around ten-thirty."

She nodded happily. "Okay," she said.

"Great. I'll introduce you to everyone—we didn't have enough time for that last Saturday. And the director told me to tell you how much he appreciated you and Maribeth working."

"Is it always that busy?" Liberty asked.

Brent's smile faded. "Not as hectic, but the line grows longer every day. There seem to be more homeless people each week. I guess they come to California to get away from the cold weather in other parts of the country, and it's becoming one of the city's biggest problems. No one really knows what to do about these people living—and dying—on the streets."

"But how do you find time for student council and all the other things you do?"

"I've had to make some compromises. I dropped basketball and track this year. I had to give up something, and sports seemed to be the most expendable thing in my life." He smiled across the table at her. "It was mostly an ego trip anyway. I have to work to earn money for college, but I never even considered giving up student council or volunteering at the shelter."

Compared to Brent, Liberty suddenly felt very shallow. "Where are you going to college?" she asked.

"State. I have a scholarship, but it still takes money, and I have two brothers already in college. My folks are about tapped out."

Admiration glowed in Liberty's brown eyes as she gazed at him. "You're pretty amazing, Brent Miller."

"Not really. As a matter of fact, this girl I

used to date broke up with me because I didn't spend enough time with her. She said I was selfish and that bothers me. Maybe I am."

Margo Thompson, Liberty thought as a pang of jealousy shot through her. She couldn't imagine anyone telling Brent he was selfish.

When they arrived back at Liberty's house, Gram was in the living room, watching a rock group on MTV. Mrs. Layton had gone to bed.

"Gram, I can't *believe* you're watching this," Liberty said.

"To be honest, I was channel-hopping and I saw this strange-looking girl with blue hair in a Viking outfit, playing some kind of an electric guitar, and I stopped to listen," Gram said. "She didn't play nearly as well as you do."

Brent turned to Liberty with a look of great surprise. "I didn't know you played the guitar, Lib."

Liberty shrugged. "A little."

"*A little!*" her grandmother repeated. "She's been trained in classical guitar since she was nine. Her father was an accomplished musician."

"I'd love to hear you play," Brent said.

"Sure," Liberty agreed. "Someday when you have time."

Brent sat down on the sofa beside Gram. "I have time now."

Uncomfortable, Liberty searched for an excuse. "It's not rock music, Brent. I don't play an electric guitar and bounce around in weird costumes. My father was a concert guitarist. I used to think that one day I might be one, too. . . ."

"Brent looks like the type of person who can appreciate classical music," Gram said. "And I haven't heard you play in ages, Lib. Get your guitar, honey."

With a deep sigh, Liberty went to her bedroom and returned with her guitar. She felt awkward about performing in front of Brent, and she wished Gram had kept quiet about her musical training.

Liberty ran her fingers over the rich wood of the instrument. "I'm a little out of practice," she confessed.

"Even out of practice, you're better than that ridiculous girl on television," Gram announced firmly.

" 'That ridiculous girl' probably makes a

couple of million a year," Liberty informed her grandmother. Then she bent her head, closed her eyes, and searched her mind for the music she wanted to play. It had been such a long time—would she remember anything at all?

She fumbled a little at first, but as Liberty became immersed in the creation of her music, she forgot about everything but the joy of coaxing forth the melody. Her slim fingers quickly regained their confidence and dexterity, and she let the magic wash over her. She began with Ravel's *Bolero*. As she felt the strings vibrate beneath her touch, she could almost see her father on the concert stage, his blond head bent low over the guitar, his eyes closed as the passionate music thrilled the audience.

When the last notes died away, Brent and Gram broke into enthusiastic applause.

Blushing, Liberty put down her guitar by the piano and sat on the bench.

"Wow!" Brent looked at her in awe. "It must be wonderful to be gifted like that! The student council is sponsoring a talent show next month. You really should enter, Lib."

Liberty shivered at the idea of performing

on a big stage with everyone in Cleveland High staring at her, waiting for her to make a mistake. "I've never played in front of a large audience. I'd be terrified," she murmured.

Gram and Brent looked at each other. "You shouldn't hide your light under a bushel, Liberty," Gram said gently.

Brent nodded. "You'll have to face your fear someday, Lib. The first time I spoke at student council I thought I'd pass out from fright, but I didn't."

She looked at him in disbelief. *Brent afraid?*

"The first time is always the worst, and then you realize fearing something is worse than facing it," he told her. "And now, I guess I'd better be getting home." Brent said good night to Liberty's grandmother. Then Liberty walked with him to his truck.

A lemon-colored moon hung over them in the cloudless sky. "I had a wonderful time," Liberty said softly.

Brent leaned toward her and tilted her chin up with his cupped hand. After staring into her eyes, he kissed her lips with a gentle caress that left her giddy.

"See you tomorrow morning," he whispered. Then he kissed her again lightly on the cheek, climbed into his pickup, and drove away.

Looking up at the moon, Liberty hugged herself in ecstasy. Brent had kissed her, and she knew she would never be the same.

Chapter Six

The next morning, Brent introduced Liberty to the staff at the Mission Pacific Shelter. Dan Roberts, the director, shook hands with her and beamed with pleasure when Brent told him that Liberty was interested in working on the weekends.

"Great, great!" He gave Brent a pat on the shoulder. To Liberty he said, "I'll let my right-hand man here explain our setup to you. I'm off to a meeting with a couple of supermarket managers. Welcome aboard, Liberty."

Slipping on his suit jacket, he ran out the door with a quick wave to Mildred Adams, the gray-haired woman who was typing at the cluttered desk closest to the door.

"Is he always like that?" Liberty asked Brent in amazement. "Going in twenty different directions?"

Brent and Mildred laughed. "Dan has only one speed and that's ninety miles an hour. This place would fall apart without him," Mildred said.

Brent then introduced Liberty to some of the other volunteers, and he took her into the kitchen. When she saw the vast amounts of food, Liberty found it hard to believe that it would all be served in a few hours.

"I never knew there were so many homeless people," she said softly.

A pained look filled Brent's eyes. "And there are so many who never make it here." He paused for a moment. "Then there are the kids. I suppose they're really why I decided to go into social work. It's bad enough to see starving kids in the Middle East on TV, but it's even worse to see them in your own city every day." Obviously embarrassed by expressing his feelings, Brent blushed and walked away to scrub the tables.

At that moment Liberty wished she could hug him. She longed to drive that sad look from his eyes.

The hours flew by for Liberty as she ladled servings of rice and beans and smiled into the vacant, often desolate eyes of the people who filed by her station. She saw Brent only occasionally as he brought the steaming tubs from the kitchen.

At two o'clock, the food was gone but the line was still coming. Liberty felt her heart sink as Dan Roberts explained to those who were waiting that they would have to come back tomorrow.

A young girl of about six stood by the entrance of the building, holding on to her father's pant leg as she gazed wistfully at the now-empty tables. Her dark eyes were haunted, all innocence long gone. When Liberty smiled at the child, the little girl gave her a hostile look before turning away.

Shaken by the girl's reaction, Liberty was still upset when she got into Brent's truck.

"She wasn't angry at you, Lib. She's angry at the world—just like her parents. Hunger can do that to you," he told her wearily.

Liberty tried to swallow past the lump in her throat. "There wasn't enough food." Her statement sounded flat, and she gazed out the window at a row of palm trees blowing in the tropical breeze.

Brent sighed. "Dan tries to keep it from happening, but sometimes there are just too many people. When donations are down, we can't buy enough food."

"I'll keep seeing that little girl's face all night," Liberty murmured.

"Don't worry, Lib. Dan probably sent those people to a church or some other organization. Sometimes he even gives them money out of his own pocket."

Liberty was surprised. "Can he afford that?"

"No. That's why he drives a ten-year-old Chevy and wears ten-year-old suits. Dan's a brilliant man—he gave up a lucrative career in law to manage the shelter. It's because he has so many contacts that we're able to feed as many people as we do. 'Dazzling Dan,' we all call him."

They both were silent for the rest of the ride, absorbed in their own thoughts about the shelter and its director.

* * *

Over the next few weeks, Liberty worked almost every Saturday at the shelter and frequently on Sundays even though Brent wasn't there. She began to see the people who passed by her as individuals, not just an anonymous group with the unfortunate label of "homeless."

Brent continued picking her up on Saturday and taking her home, but he didn't kiss her again, and he didn't ask her out for another date. She began to wonder what was wrong.

"Am I dull?" Liberty asked one Friday night when Maribeth was sleeping over at her house. "I know I don't have Margo's personality or looks, but at the shelter Brent's so sweet and friendly. And on the way home, he's attentive and polite, but that's all."

Munching on a rice cake, Maribeth watched her friend pace up and down. "Maybe he doesn't have the time, Lib. He'll be graduating soon, and he's probably got a lot on his mind."

"Too much to ask me out for a taco?" Liberty asked. "He probably regrets breaking up with Margo."

"I don't think *he* regrets it, but I think *she* does," Maribeth said. "I really shouldn't say anything, but Laura Bender said that Margo's trying to get back together with Brent. She's not as happy playing the field as she thought she would be."

Liberty felt herself sinking into a deep black hole of depression and doubt. So that was the reason Brent had been so remote over the past few weeks! He had probably heard that Margo wanted to make up, and he was waiting for her to make the first move. What a fool she had been, thinking Brent had been attracted to her!

Maribeth's news kept filtering through Liberty's mind on the ride to the shelter on Saturday morning. Although Brent was as friendly as ever, she couldn't help wondering if he was thinking about Margo.

By early afternoon her feet were aching, and her arms and shoulders were tired from the constant motion of scooping and serving food.

A hand on her shoulder startled her, and

she turned to find Brent standing at her side. His chestnut hair was damp from the steam in the kitchen, and it fell forward onto his forehead.

"I have to leave early, Lib. Can you get a ride home? I have an appointment."

Probably with Margo, she thought dismally. Liberty glanced away. "Sure. No problem, Brent. In fact, you don't have to pick me up anymore. I can walk or hitch a ride."

For a brief moment she thought she saw a hurt look in his eyes, and he removed his hand from her shoulder. "Okay, Lib. I'll see you around, then."

She watched him walk away and willed herself to hold back the tears.

After school on Monday, Liberty and Maribeth went to the city library to start research on their English term papers.

Liberty dropped her books on a vacant table and slumped into the wooden chair with a deep sigh. She glanced around the busy library. The place was packed. There were a lot of students from Cleveland, and for a moment she hoped that Brent would suddenly walk through the front door. Resting her chin in her hand, Liberty gazed into space, daydreaming. He would smile down at her, and whisk her away to a tropical island where there were no homeless people, and no Margo. They would lie on the beach all day, and she would play love songs for him on her guitar, and they would never have to worry about the future because they would always be together. . . .

Liberty heard some snickering, and her attention was captured by a group of boys laughing by the magazine section to her right. A scruffy-looking man had fallen asleep on one of the sofas and was snoring with his mouth open and his head tilted back. She saw Brad Trilley, a senior at Cleveland, slip around the side of the magazine partition and move quietly toward the old man on the sofa. He was carrying a paper cup in his hand.

Liberty watched, horrified, as Brad darted forward and poured water from the cup on the man. He awakened immediately and jumped to his feet, sputtering. He then fell forward on his face. Liberty realized that one of the other boys must have tied the old man's shoelaces together.

By the time the librarian's attention focused on the old man, Brad had disappeared behind a section of bookshelves. Everyone in the library stared at the old man as he struggled to get to his feet.

Liberty slammed down her notebook in disgust and ran to assist him. As she struggled to help him up from the floor, a security guard joined her. "I'll take over, Miss. Thank you," he said.

"His shoelaces are tied together. He'll fall again," Liberty warned the guard before she walked back to her study table.

Maribeth had returned from the microfilm files. "I'm glad you helped the poor guy, Lib. Everyone else seemed to think it was one big hilarious joke. I can't believe Brad is a senior— he acted more like a seven-year-old!"

The security guard escorted the man out of the library, and the other kids settled down to their homework, whispering and glancing occasionally at Liberty. She felt her face flush with embarrassment. "I'm going to get some books," she told Maribeth and fled behind a bookcase. Tomorrow at school everybody at Cleveland would probably be laughing about the episode, and laughing at *her* for being concerned. There weren't many people like Brent and Dan Roberts who really cared what happened to the homeless, she realized angrily.

Resting her hot forehead against the bookcase, Liberty closed her eyes. She became aware of voices on the other side of the shelves and was about to move away when she overheard a girl's voice saying, "Did you see that blonde helping that old bum?"

There was a low snicker before the answer came from her companion. "Yeah. Isn't that the new girl with the weird name that Brent Miller dated once or twice?"

"Brent must have a thing for blondes!"

At that remark they broke into giggles.

"I hear that Margo wants him back," the first girl said.

"Who wouldn't? Brent's a hunk, and he's really smart, too. I wonder why they broke up?"

"Do you think it was over that blonde with the freckles? She's only a junior, isn't she?"

"I don't think they broke up over her. Anyway, she's no competition for Margo. If Margo wants him, she'll get him, you can bet on it."

Liberty waited until it was silent behind the shelves before coming out of her hiding place. *They were right,* she thought in defeat as she searched for reference books for her report. *I'm no competition for Margo Thompson, and I must have been crazy to think Brent could ever be interested in me!*

Chapter Seven

The next day after school Liberty and Maribeth changed into their sweats and headed for the athletic field as usual. Liberty's pride still stung from the conversation she had overheard in the library, but she kept the hurt to herself, unwilling to confide even in her best friend. They began to jog slowly around the track.

"It smells like spring," Maribeth commented, sniffing the balmy air deep into her lungs.

Liberty glanced at the vivid orange and yellow flowers on the ice plant that seemed to grow everywhere in California. "How can you tell? It looks the same all the time." A stab of homesickness saddened her with a sudden ache for the lush green farmlands of Indiana.

Maribeth began coughing and had to stop jogging to catch her breath. When she could speak again, she warned Liberty, "Number one rule for surviving in California, Lib: *Don't breathe!* The pollution will get you if the freeways don't."

"I thought that brown haze I saw hanging over the mountains to the east was fog," Liberty said.

"Brown fog is smog. My mother says that wasn't here ten years ago. San Diego is such a great place—I hope it never gets as smoggy as L.A. But if people keep moving here by the thousands—" she broke off suddenly. "Oops, I didn't mean you, Lib!"

Liberty smiled. "It's all right, Maribeth. Sometimes I still wish I were back home in Indiana, but then I would never have met you." *Or Brent,* she added sadly to herself.

They resumed jogging and had completed a couple of laps when a familiar voice behind them said, "Hey, wait up!"

The runner fell in beside Liberty, and her heart lurched as she looked up at Brent.

"How did things go at the shelter Saturday after I left?" he asked her.

"Fine. We stopped serving at two-thirty. I stayed to help clean up."

Brent and Liberty stopped jogging, and Maribeth discreetly continued on by herself. They walked off the track and stood under the shade of a giant palm tree. Brent scuffed the toe of his track shoe in the dirt and cleared his throat.

"I—uh—felt like you were angry with me when I left early Saturday," he said. "I'm sorry, Lib. I have so much going on in my life that I guess I'm kind of abrupt with people sometimes. It's like I'm always running to keep from being late for my job, or the shelter, or school."

"No, I wasn't angry . . ." Liberty began, then stopped short when she saw Margo Thompson coming toward them.

Brent turned, following the focus of Liberty's gaze, and his eyes widened as Margo waved to him.

Liberty's heart sank to the toes of her

sneakers. Why did Margo have to pick this exact moment to show up with her brief shorts and an even briefer tube top? A cloud of soft blond hair framed Margo's face as she drew nearer and smiled up at Brent.

"Hi, Brent. I've been looking all over for you," Margo said as she gave Liberty a saccharine smile. "I don't believe I've been introduced to your *friend*."

Margo's stress on the word "friend" brought a glint of annoyance to Liberty's eyes.

"This is Liberty Layton. Lib, Margo Thompson." Highly uncomfortable, Brent stood between the two girls as they silently appraised each other.

"I've seen you around school," Margo said, then quickly returned her attention to Brent.

She makes me sound like one of the lockers in the hallway, Liberty thought irritably.

"Liberty also helps out at the shelter," Brent told Margo.

"Oh, yes," Margo said, giving him a high-voltage smile that revealed her perfect white teeth. "I remember—she was on TV with you."

"Liberty's an Aquarius," Brent attempted to explain. "She's also interested in humanitarian work."

"I'm not into astrology, Brent. But I *do* believe in destiny," Margo practically purred.

Yuck! Liberty thought in disgust. *If Brent falls for that line, he's not as smart as I thought he was!*

"I *did* want to talk with you about a private matter, Brent," Margo continued.

"I have to go, Brent," Liberty said. "Maribeth's waiting for me. I guess I'll see you at the shelter on Saturday."

"See you, Lib," Brent called as she stalked away.

In the locker room a short while later, Liberty did her best imitation of Margo. "I *do* believe in destiny," she said, and batted her eyelashes while Maribeth nearly collapsed in laughter on the floor.

"She actually *said* that? It sounds like something out of a corny old movie!" Maribeth went into another fit of laughter.

Liberty jammed her sweat suit into her bag. "It's so obvious what she's doing," she said through clenched teeth, "but guys are so stupid when it comes to beautiful girls." She could still see Brent's reaction when he had first seen Margo coming toward him across the field in her snug shorts and tube top.

Maribeth held the door open as Liberty struggled through with her books and bag full of jogging clothes.

"I wouldn't sell Brent short, Lib," she said. "I think he's smarter than you're giving him credit for."

Smart? Maybe, Liberty thought as their footsteps echoed through the now-silent halls of Cleveland High. *But what male alive would pick a rangy mustang when there was a flashy Thoroughbred filly prancing in the corral?*

Chapter Eight

The next morning Liberty was rushing through the hall to her English class when she literally ran into Brent coming out of the principal's office. Her books went flying across the crowded corridor, and her notebook binder came undone, causing a shower of paper to litter the hall.

"Oh, no," she groaned as hundreds of feet mangled her homework. Brent got busy retrieving her books while she tried to crawl through the tangle of rushing feet to salvage at least a portion of her homework.

The final bell sounded, and Liberty collapsed against a locker with a groan of frustration.

"I *hate* having phys ed just before English! Something like this always happens," she wailed. Her hair was still wet from the shower, and her jeans felt clammy against her damp skin.

"I think this is all your stuff, Lib," Brent said, handing her a pile of books and papers.

She sighed. "Thanks. I should have been watching where I was going."

"No harm done. See, you didn't even tear my poster." He held up a large orange flier. "It's for the talent show I told you about." He reached into a folder and pulled out a piece of paper. "And here's an entry form with all the information."

After a moment's hesitation, Liberty took the form and stuffed it into her American history book. She had forgotten all about the show.

Brent walked with her into the office where they were both given late passes.

As they started to leave the office, Brent said, "Tryouts for the show are in one week, and I'll sic your grandmother on you if you try to get out of it!" He softened his threat with a conspiratorial wink.

"I'll think about it," Liberty promised as she went on her way to class.

After school on Friday, Liberty and Maribeth went to Horton Plaza to shop for clothes. Jogging and dieting had slimmed Maribeth down, and she was eager to buy outfits that would call attention to her new figure. Liberty had tucked the fifty dollars from her grandmother into her purse just in case she found something she couldn't resist.

The popular shopping center with its multilevel, high-rise design had breathed new life into the downtown area. A wide variety of shops, restaurants, art galleries, and novelty stores drew tourists from all over southern California.

Maribeth pointed to a painting in the window of a basement-level art gallery. "Lib, look! They want thirty-five thousand dollars for that painting!"

Liberty thought of the shelter, which was just a few blocks away, and wondered how many homeless people Dan Roberts could help with thirty-five thousand dollars. "We could sure use money like that at the shelter," she said with a sigh.

"You've really become involved in that place."

"I admire Dan Roberts, and I like being a part of what he's doing."

"It doesn't hurt that Brent's there either, does it?" Maribeth chided.

"This may surprise you, Maribeth, but I've been working there on Sundays, too, and Brent never comes then." Liberty frowned. "And Margo will probably make him give up working Saturdays, too, once they're back together again."

Maribeth gave her friend a look of surprise. "I don't think anybody could make him do anything he didn't want to do—oh, look, Lib," she said, changing the subject abruptly. "There's a psychic! Let's take a look into the future."

Liberty shook her head. "I don't think I want to, Maribeth. Sometimes it's better to find things out as you go along."

"Oh, come on, Lib." She pulled Liberty over to the sign that read: PSYCHIC ADVISOR.

"I don't want to do this, Maribeth," Liberty muttered. She lowered her voice and whispered, "How much will this looking into the future cost? I don't want to throw away my birthday money on this nonsense."

"Shhh," Maribeth cautioned. "She'll hear you."

Liberty rolled her eyes in exasperation. "If she's *really* psychic, won't she know what I'm thinking anyway?"

Giving Liberty a poke in the ribs, Maribeth smiled at the woman standing in front of a white flower cart and asked, "How much for a reading?"

Liberty was fascinated by the crystal around the woman's neck. It was a rose quartz attached to a silver unicorn, and the woman constantly fondled the smooth stone.

"Ten dollars each," the woman replied.

While Maribeth sat down with the psychic, Liberty sat on a bench in front of a toy store. After a while she glanced over at Maribeth, who slid off the chair and motioned to Liberty. Liberty reluctantly got up and walked over.

"She's great," Maribeth whispered in delight. "She says a tall, good-looking guy is going to come into my life any day now!"

Liberty rolled her eyes again, but said nothing as she handed the psychic a ten-dollar bill. *She* could have predicted that Maribeth was going to have someone coming into her life before long—with her weight loss and improved self-confidence, she was attracting a lot of male attention at Cleveland.

Liberty took the seat Maribeth had just vacated. Her vision of psychics was limited to what she had seen in the movies or on TV—a mysterious woman wearing a gypsy outfit, sitting in a darkened room. But this woman was dressed in a sensible dark suit much like the ones Liberty's mother wore to work, and the sun was shining brightly.

"No crystal ball?" Liberty inquired, then blushed as she realized how condescending she sounded.

The woman's soft, throaty laughter surprised her, and so did the calm feeling that suddenly enveloped her in the midst of all the hustle and bustle around them. For a few minutes they talked about the weather, the crowd in the center, the tourists.

Suddenly the woman touched Liberty's long, slim fingers with a light, feathery caress. "You are very talented in some area of music," she said in her low, pleasant voice.

Liberty's eyes widened in surprise.

The woman closed her eyes for a moment. "You have a great deal of talent but you've been neglecting it," the psychic went on.

Liberty was glad she was sitting down because otherwise she might have fallen over. Stunned, she remained silent as the woman looked deep into her eyes and then smiled, saying, "You have an obligation to your talent, but fear is holding you back from using it. Only by facing your fear can you overcome it."

A few minutes later when Liberty and Maribeth entered an ice-cream parlor for a diet soda, Liberty's knees were still shaking.

"Well? Well?" Maribeth prompted as they sat down at a table.

"You must have told her something about me," Liberty accused.

"Lib!" Maribeth cried. "I did not!"

"I'm sorry, Maribeth. It's just that she seemed to be looking into my mind."

Maribeth smiled smugly. "That's what psychics do, dummy. Good, isn't she?"

Liberty frowned. "I don't believe in this. It's so . . . so . . ."

"California?" Maribeth finished with a giggle.

Liberty laughed, too. "That's the word I was looking for!"

"So are you going to tell me what she said or let me die of curiosity?" Maribeth demanded when Liberty said nothing else.

"Well, she talked about my musical talent and told me I was neglecting it," Liberty finally replied. "Of course, it *could* have been just a lucky guess. I mean, these fortune-tellers have to be really good at sizing people up. If I had said, 'No, I don't have any musical talent,' I bet she would have come up with something else until she hit it."

Maribeth gave her a knowing smirk. "Sure, Lib. Just a lucky guess. Right."

By eight o'clock, Maribeth had spent all her money. Liberty didn't buy anything except a box of chocolates for her mother and grandmother to share—there was nothing she really needed or wanted, and she suddenly decided to donate the money to the homeless shelter when she went there on Saturday morning. Somehow she was sure Gram wouldn't mind.

Back in Liberty's bedroom, Maribeth modeled her new jeans and three new sweaters while Liberty kept thinking of what the psychic had said. She took her guitar out of the case, sat on the bed, and began playing "Somewhere My Love."

"It almost makes me cry when you play love songs, Lib," Maribeth said. "I agree with Brent and your grandmother—you *should* enter the talent contest." She paused and looked at herself from a side angle in the mirror. "Did you play a love song that night when you played for Brent?"

Liberty shook her head. "No—just some light classical numbers."

"Well, I bet if you *did* play him a love song, he'd forget about Margo in a heartbeat," Maribeth stated.

Liberty sighed. "Don't I wish!"

Maribeth began putting her new clothes

back in their boxes. "Anyway, Lib, I'll never speak to you again if you don't enter that talent show!"

"Who won last year?"

After a brief pause, Maribeth answered with a giggle. "Margo Thompson."

Astonished, Liberty asked, "With what?"

"She sang something from *Grease,* I think. I can't remember for sure."

"Was she really good?"

"Well, her voice is a little squeaky on the high notes," Maribeth said. "But it doesn't sound too bad if you're in the back row." She started to giggle again.

But Liberty wasn't laughing. It seemed that wherever she turned, she was always competing with Margo Thompson.

With her packages in her arms, Maribeth said, "You *will* enter, won't you, Lib?"

Liberty sighed. "I don't know, Maribeth. All the kids are into rock music and rap. I'd just die if everyone laughed because they didn't understand my music."

"Lib, no one is going to laugh at a talent like yours. Maybe you could do a medley of tunes, stuff with a strong beat and a lot of fire. A lot of the acts last year were so boring, you could fall asleep."

"So what you're trying to say is, no classical?" Liberty asked.

"Not if you want to beat Margo," Maribeth answered as she dashed out the door.

Chapter Nine

Liberty had a lot to think about over the next two days. She kept hearing the psychic's words: "You have an obligation to your talent . . . but fear is holding you back . . ."

All day Sunday, she practiced her guitar, and on Monday afternoon when the last bell rang, she walked into the auditorium with her guitar case in one hand and the entry form in the other. With her heart beating violently against her rib cage, Liberty handed the form to Ms. Davis, one of the teachers in charge of the auditions, and said, "I'd like to try out for the talent show."

Ms. Davis peered over her red-framed glasses at Liberty as she took the entry form. Beside her, Mrs. Martinez, the music teacher, brightened when she saw the guitar case. "Oh, good! We need some variety. So far, we have mostly singers, dancers, and baton twirlers."

"Take a seat, Liberty," Ms. Davis said. "We'll call your name when it's your turn."

As her eyes adjusted to the dim lighting in the auditorium, Liberty saw about fifteen or twenty kids scattered around in the seats. The members of the student council judging committee were sitting in the front center row. Liberty saw Brent among them as she walked by. Her heart sank like a fallen soufflé when she saw him turn around in his seat to talk to Margo Thompson.

Nothing like trying to get in good with the judges, she thought as she chose an empty seat near the middle of the auditorium. She battled an urge to run and hide, and struggled to fight back her rising panic. Focusing her attention on the brightly lit stage, Liberty dreaded the moment when she would have to make that long walk down the aisle and up the flight of stairs.

At three-thirty, Mrs. Martinez strode to the center of the stage and announced that the auditions were about to begin.

Liberty removed her guitar from its case and took several deep breaths to calm her nerves. The first act was Randy Masters, a senior who was well-known for his pranks. Liberty felt sorry for him when his stand-up comic routine fell flat. There were a few embarrassed giggles now and then but for the most part, his jokes died a silent death as did his act.

So much for being funny on cue, Liberty thought as she watched Randy, serious for once in his life, practically run out of the auditorium. She wondered if everyone else who was waiting to try out was as nervous as she was. Pressing her palms together, she tried to keep her hands from shaking as she glanced around. Margo was again leaning over to whisper into Brent's ear.

"Give it a rest, Margo," she murmured aloud, then glanced around, wondering if anyone had heard her talking to herself.

The next act was a piano solo performed by Cindy Ho, a sophomore. As the familiar strains of Chopin's *Fantasie Impromptu* drifted through the auditorium, Liberty leaned forward in her seat. Cindy was not only good, she was great, Liberty realized. When Cindy had finished her solo, everyone broke into enthusiastic applause.

"Margo Thompson," Mrs. Martinez announced next.

Liberty watched as Margo walked confidently up the steps to the stage. Brent adjusted the microphone, and her accompanist seated himself at the piano. Then she began to sing. Liberty thought she sounded pretty decent on the first selection, but the last song was simply beyond Margo's vocal range. Now Liberty knew what Maribeth meant when she had said Margo sounded squeaky on the high notes!

As Margo beamed at the applause, Liberty realized that nobody, including Margo, was aware of her limited vocal range. Apparently it didn't matter—judging from the round of applause she had received, it was obvious that Margo would definitely be in the talent show.

After a ventriloquist, a ballet dancer, a few

more singers, and a couple of baton twirlers had done their thing, the moment Liberty had dreaded arrived.

"Liberty Layton," Mrs. Martinez announced.

Liberty picked up her guitar and started down the aisle to the stage. *Don't trip, please don't trip,* she silently begged her feet.

Brent came up on stage, set out a stool, and lowered the microphone. "Knock 'em dead, Lib," he whispered as he hurried down the steps.

Her heart pounding furiously, Liberty looked over the footlights into the darkened auditorium. She had never felt so alone—or scared—in her life. Her fingers were trembling, and the silence was overwhelming. She was sure that everyone in the front row could hear the rapid beating of her heart.

For one awful moment, Liberty drew a complete blank. What was she going to play? Could she remember? She bit her lip in concentration as she placed her fingers on the strings. The familiar motion released Liberty from her paralysis, and she launched into a vibrant Spanish flamenco medley that resonated throughout the auditorium.

When she finished, there was absolute silence. Liberty's heart sank. She had played her best, but she had failed. With tears stinging her eyes, she rose from the stool, intent on finding her way off the stage as quickly as possible. Suddenly she heard applause, and she noticed that the student judges and both teachers were giving her a standing ovation.

As Liberty came down the steps clutching her guitar, Brent met her and hugged her.

"I knew you could do it!" he said. "I never doubted it for a moment!"

Then the other members of the audition committee gathered around her, asking questions and praising her performance. But even as Liberty basked in the glow of this unexpected admiration, she looked past the beaming faces to the dark seats beyond the first row, and a new fear was born.

She had managed to overcome her stage fright in an almost empty auditorium. But what would happen on the night of the talent show when the place was filled with hundreds of people?

Chapter Ten

Liberty was still glowing from the success of her performance when she met Maribeth at her locker after school on Tuesday.

"All I could hear all over school today," Maribeth said, "was how great you were at the audition. And you weren't even going to try out!"

"I was scared to death," Liberty admitted as she waited for Maribeth. They had decided to skip their usual jogging routine in order to work on their term papers.

"But you did it, Lib. I'm really proud of

you." She peered into the small mirror glued to the inside of her locker door and ran a brush through her short curls.

Maribeth had just shut the locker door when somebody called out, "Hey, Maribeth."

Liberty and Maribeth turned to see Patrick O'Brien coming down the hall, carrying his jacket and a couple of books. "Hi, Liberty," he said. "Uh—Maribeth, are you going to the library to work on your term paper?"

Maribeth nodded. "Afraid so. I'm not making much progress with it so far."

"I'd be happy to drive you," Pat offered eagerly. "Maybe later we could stop someplace for a quick snack."

Maribeth's face lit up, and she and Pat turned to look at Liberty as though suddenly remembering her presence.

"Yeah, Lib. You can come, too, I guess," Pat said as an unenthusiastic afterthought.

Liberty squeezed Maribeth's shoulder. "You guys go ahead. I think I'll skip the library tonight—gotta practice my guitar."

Smiling, Liberty watched her best friend walk down the hall with Pat O'Brien, and realized that she would probably be seeing a lot less of Maribeth in the future.

Later that evening she was sitting on her bed, studying a guitar arrangement when her mother came into the room.

"I thought you and Maribeth were going to be working on your term papers at the library tonight."

"We were, but Maribeth has just been discovered by the opposite sex," Liberty told her. "I never should have helped her lose weight!"

Mrs. Layton sat on the foot of the bed. "Has she lost that much already?"

Liberty grinned. "Enough to give her confidence. That's all she really needed. I'm going to miss her, but it was time for a change. Only now she's going to swear it's because that fortune-teller told her a tall, good-looking guy would be coming into her life!"

"Speaking of changes, Lib, are you still homesick?" her mother asked.

Her fingers strummed the guitar strings softly. "Sometimes, I guess. Only now when I think of Smithdale and my old friends, I'm starting to feel like it's somebody I used to be. And when I'm at the shelter, I look at those people and realize they don't know what homesick is because they don't have any homes to miss."

Mrs. Layton breathed a compassionate sigh. "My little girl is growing up."

"Brent said the shelter would help me sort out my values in a hurry. . . ."

"How is Brent?" her mother asked. "Gram and I thought he was so nice."

Liberty blushed. "Oh, he's fine. He and Gram practically forced me to enter the talent contest, you know." She smiled, remembering his warm embrace after the audition.

"You really like him, don't you?"

Coming back to reality, Liberty said, "Yeah, but so does Margo Thompson."

At lunch the next day Liberty was listening to Maribeth describe her date with Pat, when she looked up to see Margo heading for their table.

Maribeth nearly choked on her tuna sandwich as Margo stopped and smiled at Liberty, her blue eyes like chips of ice.

"I understand you did rather well at the audition Monday," Margo said. "I'm sorry I didn't wait around to hear you."

Liberty continued to chew a carrot stick as she waited for Margo to go on.

"We seem to be bumping into each other a lot lately."

"So it seems," Liberty agreed, taking a sip of her milk.

"For your information, I intend to win first prize in the talent show again this year," Margo said sweetly. "I plan on a career in musical theater, and another award will make a nice entry on my résumé."

"Are you suggesting that I withdraw so there will be less competition?" Liberty asked just as sweetly.

Margo smirked at her. "I'm saying, Liberty *dear*, that a different panel of judges selects the winners of the actual competition. And they all happen to be good friends of mine. Besides, a vocalist stands a much better chance of winning than an instrumentalist anyway. Look at the Miss America contest."

"Are you planning on entering that, too?" Maribeth asked with interest.

Margo's disdainful glance swept over Maribeth and dismissed her as unworthy of her attention. "And Liberty," she added as she turned to walk away, "I wouldn't count on seeing Brent at the shelter too much longer. He'll soon be spending all his Saturdays with me."

"Of all the—" Maribeth sputtered as Margo stalked to the other side of the cafeteria to join her friends.

"I believe that girl wants to win," Liberty commented in a droll tone. "In more ways than one!" she added grimly.

"Lib, you just *have* to win that contest!"

Liberty sighed. "The odds are becoming worse every minute, Maribeth. Now I not only have to contend with my stage fright, but I have to face a judging committee made up of Margo's friends."

"That's probably how she won last year," Maribeth said, scowling.

"Maybe I should withdraw."

"Don't you dare, Lib! You're ten times as good as Margo."

Liberty threw her head back, tossing her hair dramatically. "Then it's destiny, dahling," she said in a fair imitation of Margo. Maribeth went into a fit of giggling.

Although she joined in the laughter, Liberty wasn't at all sure she had made the right decision.

On her way to French class that afternoon, Liberty met Brent in the hall.

"It's supposed to rain Saturday. How about me picking you up?" he suggested.

As she gazed into his eyes, Liberty thought of Margo's threat. Apparently she hadn't yet persuaded him to give up his work at the shelter.

"Sure," Liberty agreed with a bright smile.

"Be there around ten-thirty," he promised, then rushed off to beat the final bell.

"You're not going to win this one, Margo *dahling*," Liberty muttered as she rushed into French class.

Chapter Eleven

"You were really great at that audition, Lib," Brent said on Saturday morning as they headed for the shelter. The sky over San Diego was gray and overcast with the imminent threat of rain.

"Thanks," Liberty said with a smile. "But that was just an audition, not the real thing. I get goose bumps even thinking about that."

"You'll win," he predicted with confidence.

Not if Margo has her way, Liberty thought. "Just exactly how is the winner picked?" she asked in what she hoped was a casual manner.

Brent pulled the truck into a parking space next to Dan Roberts' old Chevy. "A committee of four teachers and six student council members make the final decision. Of course, they're influenced by the audience response, but I think that's only right, don't you?"

Liberty nodded as they walked into the shelter. Margo had neglected to mention that there were teachers on the committee, and Liberty suspected that dear Margo had been trying to undermine her already shaky confidence. "Will you be one of the judges?"

"No, because I was on the audition panel." Brent grinned as he held the door. "But if I were, I'd vote for you, Lib, because you're the best."

The line seemed never ending as Liberty ladled rice and beans onto the parade of plates moving constantly by her station. She tried to give everyone a smile along with the serving of hot food.

The older people who came through the line were apt to return her smile, but many of the younger ones seemed bewildered, as though they couldn't figure out who to blame for their homelessness and hunger.

Both Brent and Dan Roberts had warned Liberty about the need to avoid emotional involvement, but she knew it was difficult even for Dan to remain detached when he saw so many in dire need.

"Just think of the warm meal you're giving them," Brent had told her, and Liberty tried to focus on the positive side—she was helping to bring a tiny ray of sunshine into lives darkened by the constant gloom of poverty.

As she scooped up the last of the rice, Liberty looked up and saw a teenage girl waiting silently with an empty plate. "It'll just be a second," she promised. "Brent, I need more rice," she yelled toward the kitchen. Liberty smiled at the girl, who looked to be about her own age, but there was no response. The girl wore grimy jeans and a wrinkled blouse that hung beneath the uneven hem of her faded blue sweater. Liberty's eyes came to rest on the thin hands with their dirty nails, and she looked down at her own clean, polished nails with a feeling of guilt.

Then she noticed a younger girl standing next to the teenager. She too was waiting anxiously for the arrival of more food from the kitchen.

"Is that your sister?" Liberty asked the teenager.

The older girl nodded. Liberty was relieved when Brent came hurrying in with another huge vat of rice, and she added an extra dollop of rice and beans to both girls' plates.

When the serving line finally shut down for the day, Liberty hurried outside to throw away some of the trash. A cold drizzle was starting to fall, and she shivered as she lugged the big plastic bags to the bin behind the shelter.

She had just lifted the lid when a cough caught her attention, and she turned to see the two girls to whom she had given the extra portions of food, sitting on the ground behind the trash bin. Liberty wondered if they had been going through the garbage before she came out of the building. Brent had told her about finding people sleeping in the huge trash bins. Even in southern California, the February nights were cool, and transients took refuge wherever they could. As she bent down to pick up the trash bags, Liberty saw the older girl's feet. The soles of her ragged sneakers had pulled away from

108

the fabric and her bare toes were sticking out.

The rain was coming down more heavily now, and a cold wind began to whip along the alley.

"If you need a place to stay, I can tell Mr. Roberts, and he'll find shelter for you and your sister," Liberty said.

The older girl took her sister's hand, and they stood up and started to inch away from Liberty. She realized they were afraid of her. They probably were running away from something, Liberty decided, and she hated to think what it might be.

"Wait!" Liberty called as they tried to edge past her and make a break for the street.

Alerted to the urgency in Liberty's voice, the girls stopped and stared at her like cornered animals.

"Take these—they look like they'll fit." Liberty quickly unlaced her expensive new sneakers, slipped them off, and handed them to the older girl. The girl couldn't seem to believe her eyes. When Liberty nodded encouragingly, she put the shoes on her dirty feet and tied the laces, all the while glancing up at Liberty as though she were afraid Liberty might change her mind and take them back.

Liberty pulled some change out of her jeans pocket and handed the coins to the younger girl.

"Thanks," the older girl called over her shoulder as she pulled her sister toward the street.

Liberty watched them walk downtown, turning around every few steps to look back at her. She stood looking after them until she became aware of her own wet feet. Then she picked up the girl's old sneakers and tossed them into the trash bin.

As Liberty hurried back inside the shelter, her wet socks squished on the tile floor.

"Brent," she called as he came out of the kitchen, "could you give me a ride home? I just gave away my shoes, and I think my mother is probably going to kill me."

Chapter Twelve

On the drive to Liberty's house, Brent turned the truck heater on high so her wet socks could dry.

"I didn't think about the consequences or what my mother would say," she told him. "At the time, all I could think of was I *had* to help somehow."

Brent's eyes were serious as he studied her worried face. "That's the kind of thing Dan would do." He reached over and pushed a wet strand of hair back from her face. "Maybe I shouldn't have gotten you involved in the shelter. You may be too sensitive," he said, choosing his words with the utmost care. "To be an effective social worker, you have to be able to stay emotionally detached."

"Like Dan?" she said and they both laughed.

"Well, Dan is an exception, but don't forget he wasn't really trained in social work to begin with. And you know what? I found out he's an Aquarius just like you, Lib," Brent added with a grin.

He pulled to a stop in front of her building, and Liberty started to get out. "Wait, Lib. I'll come with you—I don't want you to face your mother alone."

"Thanks, Brent," she said.

He smiled down at her as they walked along the sidewalk. "What are friends for if they can't help you when you're in trouble?"

Friends? Liberty thought. Her heart sank. Brent had never given her any indication that they were anything else. That one kiss in the moonlight was obviously just a friendly gesture. The lump in her throat grew until she thought it would choke her.

Liberty's mother and Gram were in the living room, watching television. Mrs. Layton looked up in surprise when she saw Brent come in with Liberty, and then she looked down in amazement at Liberty's wet socks.

"Your daughter gave her shoes away to a homeless girl," Brent announced before Liberty could offer an explanation.

Mrs. Layton looked horrified, but Gram smiled.

Her mother gasped. "Your birthday shoes?"

Liberty nodded and looked down at the carpet.

"I feel like it's partially my fault, Mrs. Layton," Brent said quickly.

Liberty listened as he explained what had happened at the shelter. *Why is Gram smiling?* she wondered vaguely. Then she heard Brent say, "I have to run to make it to my job." He turned to Liberty. "If I don't get a chance to talk to you in school this week, Lib, I'll be rooting for you in the talent contest on Friday."

She gave him a numb smile and walked with him to the door.

When Brent had left, the silence in the living room was thick with tension.

"I can't *believe* you actually gave your new

shoes away!" her mother finally managed to say.

"I'm sorry, Mom. I just couldn't help it," Liberty mumbled.

"Liberty," her grandmother said softly, "could you go to your room for a few minutes? I want to talk to your mother in private. And take off those wet socks, dear, before you get a cold."

Oh, boy, I did it again, Liberty thought as she shut her bedroom door and took off her socks. She'd disappointed her mother and now, as usual, Gram was going to try to save her skin. Her mother would probably ground her for life for doing such a stupid thing.

Liberty took her guitar out of the closet. As she idly strummed, she wiggled her bare toes and decided that deep in her heart, she was glad she had given the shoes away. She would wear her old sneakers until she could save up enough money to replace them. She could even get a part-time job—it was time for her to start helping with the family finances. She wasn't a little kid anymore.

Liberty looked up apprehensively as the bedroom door opened. Her mother came in carrying a large box which she placed on the foot of the bed.

"I'm sorry, Mom," Liberty said. "It wasn't a bright thing to do—I guess I was thinking with my heart instead of my head."

Then she noticed that her mother had tears in her eyes.

"I'm so proud of you!" Mrs. Layton said.

Liberty blinked in amazement. "I thought you'd ground me until I was ninety!"

Her mother wiped her eyes. "I *was* angry at first, but your grandmother set me straight. She made me realize something very important about possessions, which you've evidently already learned."

Liberty gazed at her mother in bewilderment.

"You gave away your shoes because someone else needed them," Mrs. Layton went on. "And that unselfish act opened my eyes, as well as my heart. Open the box, Lib."

Liberty peeled away the tape that held the lid on to the box. When she lifted the lid she gasped.

"Go ahead," her mother urged. "Take it out."

Sudden tears blinded Liberty as she reverently lifted the beautiful guitar that had been her father's. She stroked the wood with trembling fingers.

"You see, Liberty, sometimes parents can learn from their children, too," Mrs. Layton said softly. "The guitar belongs to you—it should have been yours all along. I want you to play it in the talent show. I guess I thought I was preserving your father's memory by keeping it packed away, but I was wrong. The best possible tribute to him is for you to make music with this guitar the way he did. We're only truly alive when we can bring pleasure into someone else's life."

"Are you sure, Mom?" Liberty asked.

Her mother nodded. "I'm sure."

Liberty put the guitar on the bed and gave her mother a huge hug. For a long moment they clung together. At last Mrs. Layton moved away and said with a tremulous smile, "That's the good news. And now for the bad news, Lib." In response to Liberty's questioning expression, she continued, "I can't be here Friday night for the talent show." She sighed. "My boss called this afternoon and told me I have to be in Atlanta on Thursday for a series of interviews. I'm so sorry, Lib, but Gram will be there. And I'll be thinking about you every single minute, pulling for you to win."

Liberty was disappointed, but instead of turning on her mother with anger and recriminations as she would once have done, she forced a smile. "It's okay, Mom. I understand, really I do. I know you'd be there if you could."

Mrs. Layton touched her cheek gently. "My little girl really *has* grown up," she said.

Later that night as Liberty sat in her bedroom, tuning her dad's guitar, she discovered that the anger she had harbored for so long was completely gone.

It had come as a shock to discover that life was a growing and learning experience for her mother just as it was for her. And Gram had helped heal the rift between Liberty and her mother once and for all.

Gram, you wonder worker! Liberty thought. *I wish you could wave your magic wand and make Brent love me instead of Margo Thompson!*

Chapter Thirteen

As she stood in the wings of the Cleveland High auditorium on Friday night, Liberty watched Cindy Ho play her piano solo. She fiddled nervously with her gold-trimmed brown velvet vest until Maribeth, who had come backstage to offer moral support, hissed, "Stop it, Lib! You're making *me* nervous, and *I* don't even have to go out there!"

"Are you sure I look all right?" Liberty felt strange in her long floral skirt and brown suede boots instead of her usual well-worn jeans and sneakers.

"You look terrific," Maribeth assured her.

Liberty glanced over at Margo, who was wearing a white sequined dress, and sighed.

But even Margo wasn't her usual cool self, Liberty observed. She was biting her thumbnail as she discussed a last-minute change in her act with the accompanist.

Cindy Ho finally finished and took a bow to tumultuous applause. As she ran into the wings she said, "The place is packed! I was so nervous."

Liberty wished *she* had just finished, but she was scheduled to follow Margo.

Titters of laughter from the audience caught her attention, and she looked onstage. Doreen Swanson, a slightly overweight sophomore, was performing a ballet selection, and she seemed to be having trouble.

"They're laughing at the poor girl," Maribeth said in a horrified whisper.

Liberty watched the girl in the white ruffled tutu and satin ballet slippers flounder around on stage. Her prerecorded music was playing at the wrong speed, and Mrs. Martinez frantically tried to adjust the record player without further disrupting Doreen's number. The laughter from the audience was growing louder.

Liberty felt beads of perspiration break out on her forehead. She felt terribly sorry for Doreen, knowing how awful she herself would feel if everyone laughed at her act. Liberty looked away from the performance, wishing that Ms. Davis would close the curtain and put Doreen out of her misery. As Liberty's eyes met Margo's, she didn't miss the smile on Margo's face. Margo's smile seemed to say: One less to compete against.

Mrs. Martinez finally got the record going at the right speed, and Doreen finished her dance, then rushed backstage with tears streaming down her face.

"Don't cry, Doreen. It wasn't that bad," Mrs. Martinez said, trying to console the sobbing girl.

"You're next, Margo," Ms. Davis whispered as the emcee, Randy Masters, wound up one of his jokes.

Margo's blue eyes narrowed. "No way! I'm not following that disaster. Let someone else go next."

Mrs. Martinez gave Margo a withering glare.

"You either perform or drop out of the contest, Margo. Randy is announcing your name now."

Furious, Margo thrust her music at her accompanist and stomped out onstage, just as her name was called.

"That girl is impossible," Mrs. Martinez muttered. "Liberty, you're next. That is, if you don't have any objections," she added sarcastically.

"No, ma'am," Liberty replied quickly.

Mrs. Martinez gave her a sheepish grin. "Sorry, Liberty. That just slipped out. I'm so tired of prima donnas! Every year I swear I'll never do another one of these talent shows, and then I always do."

Liberty and Maribeth turned their attention to Margo, who was performing center stage.

"She sounds pretty good," Liberty whispered.

"Yeah—her voice has only cracked twice so far," Maribeth whispered back.

As Margo finished her song, there was a huge wave of applause, and Liberty felt fear clutching her throat. Now it was her turn.

Gripping her father's guitar in one hand,

she squeezed Maribeth's fingers with the other as she waited for her cue. When she heard her name, Liberty stepped out onto the stage. She saw the sea of faces staring up at her, and for one horrible moment, Liberty thought she was going to faint. It was so quiet that she could hear the breathing of the audience and an occasional cough as she settled herself on her stool, trying desperately to still the frantic pounding of her heart.

As she fingered the frets with her left hand, Liberty looked out over the footlights. She could hardly believe what she saw. There, right in the front row, sat Brent, Gram, and her mother!

Joy flowed through Liberty like an electric current. Her mother had made it after all! Her delight banished the nervous tremors, and she closed her eyes, letting herself become one with the music. She played for the memory of her father, the love of her mother and grandmother, and what might have been with Brent. As the passionate strains of *Fandango de Huelva* resonated to the highest rows of the balcony, her fingers moved faster and more skillfully than they ever had before.

When the last note died away, Liberty stood up, her chin held high, and smiled at the audience with a newborn confidence, aware that she had never performed better in her life. She knew she would never again be terrified of performing.

The applause came in huge, sweeping crescendos and continued after the curtain had closed.

"Open the curtain again," Ms. Davis ordered, and pushed Liberty back onstage. "Liberty, take another bow!"

Bowing, she saw her mother weeping, and she knew the tears were for the memory of her father, whose brilliant musical career had ended far too soon. When she finally ran offstage for the final time, her own vision was blinded by tears as well.

"You were awesome, Lib," Maribeth said, giving her a hug.

Mrs. Martinez was smiling. "Now I remember why I put up with all these tantrums and unexpected disasters—because every once in a great while, I discover true talent. Congratulations, Liberty."

Liberty blushed at the praise and murmured her appreciation.

"Liberty, I can't believe you're not taking any music classes," Mrs. Martinez went on. "I checked your schedule the other day after the audition, and I simply couldn't understand it."

Liberty smiled. "That's a long story. I'll tell you later, Mrs. Martinez. But you can bet I'll be enrolled in every music course next year!"

As they stood backstage waiting for the remaining acts to be over, Liberty peered around the curtain for a quick peek at the selection committee, and discovered that three of the senior girls were Margo's lunch buddies.

Whatever will be, will be, she told herself. It didn't matter anymore whether she won first prize or even placed. It had already been a wonderful evening.

At last everyone had performed, and Liberty clutched Maribeth's hand as they waited for Randy to announce the winners.

"Third place, Ralph Washington."

Liberty and Maribeth patted Ralph on the back as he ran onstage to receive his trophy.

"Second place, Margo Thompson."

Margo pasted a big, phony smile on her

face as she waltzed to center stage to collect her prize.

Randy looked down at the list in his hand. "And the first prize winner of the Tenth Annual Cleveland High Talent Show is . . ." He paused dramatically. *"Liberty Layton!"*

"Oh, Lib," Maribeth shouted, jumping up and down. "You did it! You won. *You won!*"

As if in a trance, Liberty walked across the stage to accept her trophy. As the other performers joined her for a collective bow, she was sure she would awaken in a moment and find it had all been a dream.

After the show when Liberty joined her mother and grandmother out front, she was surprised to find Dan Roberts with them.

"Dan, I didn't know you were coming!" she cried.

He hugged Liberty and congratulated her. "Brent practically threatened to boycott the shelter if I didn't make it," he said, laughing.

"Where *is* Brent?" Mrs. Layton asked, looking around the dwindling crowd. "He was right here a second ago."

Ms. Davis, who was on her way out of the auditorium paused and said, "Brent Miller? I saw him backstage talking to Margo Thompson."

In the midst of her triumph, it was as though a dark cloud had settled over Liberty. *Well,* she thought, swallowing the hurt, *it's obvious that Brent thinks it's more important to console Margo for losing first place than to congratulate me for winning. After all, I'm only a friend.*

At the pizza party afterward, Liberty managed to keep smiling as people kept coming over to tell her how much they had enjoyed her performance. She knew she would never feel like an outsider at Cleveland High again.

Next to her, Maribeth and Pat were gazing into each other's eyes, oblivious to everyone else. And Liberty was interested to see that her mother and Dan Roberts seemed to be hitting it off very well.

"Tell me more about your job, Margery," Dan said, moving closer to Mrs. Layton.

Margery? They had just met and already it was Margery! Liberty and Gram exchanged knowing smiles

If only Brent would come, she thought.

Tonight would be perfect if he were here to help her celebrate the biggest success of her life. But although Liberty watched the entrance to the restaurant all evening, neither Brent nor Margo showed up.

I may have won the contest, Liberty thought sadly, *but Margo won the real prize—Brent's heart.*

Chapter Fourteen

"I stopped by your house, Lib, but your mother said you'd already left for the shelter," Brent said the following morning.

Liberty looked up from filling the paper napkin dispenser at the counter. "Hi, Brent," she said, trying to keep her tone casual and relaxed—like a friend. "I thought the walk would do me good. Maribeth and I have slacked off on our jogging lately. With the contest and all . . ." Her voice trailed off.

Brent moved closer to her. "I'm sorry that I didn't get a chance to congratulate you last night."

"That's okay. I understand," Liberty said quickly. Of course she understood. It was more important for him to be with Margo. After all, Liberty was just a friend.

"I don't think you do. I had to see someone because I wanted to explain about my feelings once and for all, and . . ."

"Brent, we need you in the kitchen right now," Mildred called from the doorway.

"Talk to you later," he promised as he hurried to see what the problem was.

Later when Brent joined Liberty at the serving counter, he said, "I heard that Dan made it to the show."

"Yes," Liberty replied. "He and my mother seemed to be having a really good time together."

Suddenly she heard a high, feminine voice saying, "So *this* is where you spend your time, Brent! I can't say that I see what's so intriguing about it. It certainly can't be the scenery!"

Liberty and Brent looked up in surprise as Margo Thompson, blue eyes blazing, shoved her way to the head of the line of people patiently waiting for a meal.

Liberty concentrated on filling plates with rice and vegetables. *What on earth is Margo doing here?* she wondered.

Now Margo marched around the counter to confront Brent face-to-face.

"I will never understand you, Brent Miller! How can you possibly prefer the company of these—these *derelicts* to me!" she screeched, and Liberty cringed. "I could pretend to be interested in all of this the way Liberty does," Margo went on, "but frankly, I don't think it's worth the effort."

"I thought we got this all settled last night, Margo," Liberty heard Brent say. "And for your information, Liberty isn't pretending. She really understands how I feel about wanting to make the world a better place, and *she* feels the same way!"

"How nice for you both," Margo sneered. "Well, if that's the way you feel about it, all I can say is you deserve each other!" With that, she turned on her heel and stormed out of the shelter.

Stunned by Margo's dramatic entrance and exit, Liberty tried to unravel what it all meant, and a tiny glimmer of hope began to glow in the dark place that had once been her heart.

"Brent, what . . ." she started to say, but he shook his head.

"Tell you about it later," he said. "Right now, we've got a lot of hungry people to feed."

When they had finally finished their work, Liberty and Brent got into the truck. Brent had suggested that they drive to the beach for a long, private talk, but first they stopped by Liberty's house so she could pick up a sweater and tell her mother where she was going.

"And how about getting your guitar, Lib?" Brent said. "I'd love to hear you play something just for me."

The glimmer of hope grew brighter and stronger now. Liberty could hardly wait to hear what Brent had to say.

A short while later, they were sitting on a blanket, watching a few surfers in wet suits ride the waves.

"About you and Margo . . ." Liberty began, but Brent silenced her by placing a finger against her lips.

"That's all over," he told her. "The reason I didn't come to the party last night was I was trying to make her understand that I didn't want to get back together with her. I thought she got the picture, but apparently she didn't, or she wouldn't have showed up at the shelter today." Brent bent his head and gently brushed Liberty's lips with his own, making her heart race with happiness. "You're the one I really care about, Lib," he murmured.

"But you only asked me out once," Liberty reminded him.

Brent shrugged. "I guess maybe I was afraid you'd be like Margo, demanding all my time and nagging me a lot."

Liberty's eyebrows shot up in indignation, and Brent laughed, pulling her into his arms. "But when you started working at the shelter every weekend, I found out that you were concerned about other people the same way I was. When I was with you, I didn't have to pretend to be somebody I wasn't." He kissed her again. "And then when you gave away your new shoes, I was a goner for sure!"

Liberty laughed, resting her head against

his shoulder. "I wish I'd given them away sooner!"

Serious now, Brent looked into her eyes. "How about it, Lib? Do you think you could stand going steady with a guy who'll always be a little out of step with the rest of the crowd?"

Liberty's heart was so full of joy that she couldn't speak, so she just nodded.

For a long time they sat wrapped in each other's arms, watching the sea gulls swoop over the turbulent ocean. At last, Brent said softly, "Someday, Lib, when you're a famous guitarist, promise me you'll do a concert to benefit the homeless."

"I promise," she whispered, "if you'll come to hear me."

Brent smiled at her tenderly. "I'll always come to hear you perform." Then he reached for her guitar case, opened it, and handed her the instrument. "But right now, I want a private concert, Lib. Play me a love song."

We hope you enjoyed reading this book. If you would like to receive further information about available titles in the Bantam series, just write to the address below, with your name and address: Kim Prior, Bantam Books, 61–63 Uxbridge Road, Ealing, London W5 5SA.

If you live in Australia or New Zealand and would like more information about the series, please write to:

Sally Porter   Kiri Martin
Transworld Publishers   Transworld Publishers (NZ) Ltd
(Australia) Pty Ltd   3 William Pickering Drive
15–23 Helles Avenue   Albany
Moorebank   Auckland
NSW 2170   NEW ZEALAND
AUSTRALIA

All Bantam and Young Adult books are available at your bookshop or newsagent, or can be ordered from the following address: Corgi/Bantam Books, Cash Sales Department, PO Box 11, Falmouth, Cornwall, TR10 9EN.

Please list the title(s) you would like, and send together with a cheque or postal order to cover the cost of the book(s) plus postage and packing charges of £1.00 for one book, £1.50 for two books, and an additional 30p for each subsequent book ordered to a maximum of £3.00 for seven or more books.

(The above applies only to readers in the UK, and BFPO)

Overseas customers (including Eire), please allow £2.00 for postage and packing for the first book, an additional £1.00 for a second book, and 50p for each subsequent title ordered.

First love . . . first kiss!

A terrific series that focuses firmly on that most important moment in any girl's life – falling in love for the very first time ever.

Available from wherever Bantam paperbacks are sold!

1. HEAD OVER HEELS by Susan Blake
2. LOVE SONG by Suzanne Weyn
3. FALLING FOR YOU by Carla Bracale
4. THE PERFECT COUPLE by Helen Santori

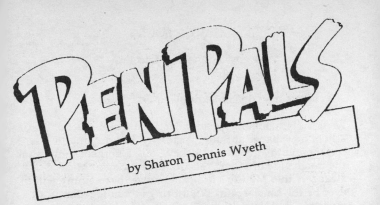

PEN PALS

by Sharon Dennis Wyeth

How do four boy-crazy girls meet four girl-crazy boys?
They place an ad for PEN PALS, of course! Well, that's what
Lisa, Shanon, Amy and Palmer (otherwise known as the
Foxes) do – and it's not long before they get a reply!

1. BOYS WANTED
2. TOO CUTE FOR WORDS
3. P.S. FORGET IT!
4. NO CREEPS NEED APPLY
5. SAM THE SHAM
6. AMY'S SONG
7. HANDLE WITH CARE
8. SEALED WITH A KISS

HART & SOUL

by Jahnna N. Malcolm

A dynamic new detective duo!

Beautiful, intelligent Amanda Hart, editor-in-chief of the school newspaper at Sutter Academy, has nothing in common with streetwise Mickey Soul, a gorgeous guy from the tough side of town. Yet, from the moment Mick swaggers into Mandy's life, she knows that nothing will ever be the same again! What brings them together is a mystery – but what keeps them together is purely a matter of heart and soul.

A contemporary, sophisticated series that is full of suspense.

1. KILL THE STORY
2. PLAY DEAD
3. SPEAK NO EVIL
4. GET THE PICTURE
5. TOO HOT TO HANDLE
6. SIGNED, SEALED, DELIVERED